About the Author

Blair Wylie is a retired Canadian oil and gas engineer and manager. He worked thirty-five years in several interesting places, including the Canadian Arctic, Western Siberia, the North Sea, Newfoundland, and Trinidad and Tobago. In his second career as a writer, he strives to entertain a thinking person. He prefers to stay in the plausible world with respect to science and character studies. His stories place people in awkward situations, and they discover hidden strengths. He hopes readers will come away feeling better about themselves, and about the future in general.

ZONT-2 AND BEYOND

*Special thanks to my brother Douglas,
who shared a gem of an idea with me...*

Blair Wylie

ZONT-2 and Beyond

Vanguard Press

VANGUARD PAPERBACK
© Copyright 2022
Blair Wylie

The right of Blair Wylie to be identified as author of
this work has been asserted by him in accordance with the
Copyright, Designs and Patents Act 1988.

All Rights Reserved

No reproduction, copy or transmission of this publication
may be made without written permission.
No paragraph of this publication may be reproduced,
copied or transmitted save with the written permission of the publisher, or in
accordance with the provisions
of the Copyright Act 1956 (as amended).
Any person who commits any unauthorised act in relation to
this publication may be liable to criminal
prosecution and civil claims for damages.

A CIP catalogue record for this title is
available from the British Library.
ISBN 978-1-80016-536-6

Vanguard Press is an imprint of
Pegasus Elliot MacKenzie Publishers Ltd.
www.pegasuspublishers.com
First Published in 2022

Vanguard Press
Sheraton House Castle Park
Cambridge England
Printed & Bound in Great Britain

Books by the Author

The *Master Defiance* Series:
Wolf Slayer
Martian Hermitage
Master Defiance
Tube Dwellers
Tube Survivors
Covert Alliance

The Perils of Isolation

ZONT-2 and Beyond

1

Bertrand Latimore, the National Security Advisor to the President of the United States, was the last to arrive in the large conference room. The plush, green leather furniture and dark, oiled wood panelling gave the place the feel of an old English gentlemen's club, although both genders were equally represented around the long table that took up most of the available space.

Bertrand emphatically motioned for everyone to stay seated as they started to scramble to their feet. "I'm really sorry I'm late, folks, and thanks for your patience, everyone." He grinned sheepishly as he wiped his brow with a neatly folded, white handkerchief. As he took his seat at the middle of the table, he confided, "The Commander-in-Chief pressed me a little longer and a little harder than usual today. She put me through a bit of a grilling. It seems she likes to do that more and more these days, with the dangerous and declining state the world is in. I don't blame her for being frustrated that we cannot always provide solid, supportable answers to her excellent questions. But back to our business at hand. First, Margaret, what's this last-minute, additional, and what you termed 'most urgent', agenda item? Your email was a bit on the cryptic side, I must say."

Margaret Dabrowski was the Director of the CIA. She was sitting directly across from Bertrand with the broad expanse of the highly polished, mahogany table between them. She adjusted her professorial looking, wire-rimmed glasses, then pulled a single page document out of a thin leather valise. It was full of bullet points that she knew by heart. She was a meticulous researcher and an obsessive planner. She noted that everyone in the room was now staring at her intently. But she was never fazed by such peer scrutiny. She knew she was perceived as competent, always prepared, and deserving of their full attention.

"A rather concerning update for you, sir," Margaret began with a clear, strong voice. "If you recall, we've been wondering what an allegedly benevolent Russian oligarch, Mister Timofey Semenov, has been up to at the Earth-Solar L1 point."

"Ah, okay… and what's this L1 deal again? And please, it's *Bert*, right? We're all old friends here, *right?*"

"Right… Bert. The L1 I'm referring to is the Lagrange One point, or the gravitational null point, between the Earth and the Sun. The Sun is about three-hundred and thirty thousand times more massive than the Earth, so the null point is a lot closer to the Earth than to the Sun. In fact, L1 is only about one percent of the distance from the Earth to the Sun. Still, that places it almost one-and-a-half million kilometres away from us, so it's a bit of a challenge logistically to get there, to say the least. But it's *worth* getting there. It's been a very useful spot in space to place satellites for observing both the Earth and the Sun. Both celestial objects appear stationary from that vantage point, except for their axial rotation of course. And also, of course, L1 orbits the Sun just like the Earth does."

"Okay, thanks. So, what about Tim's latest antics, exactly?"

"Well, as you know, he's a rather secretive chap, or *chelovek* in Russian, even with the Kremlin. We know that over the last couple of years, since, ah, March of 2036, he's commissioned several secretive, unmanned shuttle runs to L1 from his rather large, mid-Earth-orbit, experimental, manufacturing station. And suddenly, we're seeing a relatively large, perfectly-square structure at L1, albeit our optical imagery is a bit blurry from so far away."

"Really, how large?"

"We think it's about two hundred metres a side, and it's pretty thin, maybe in the order of a metre thick. The planar surface is oriented at right angles to the imaginary line between the Earth and the Sun, and at L1 it can stay that way, with a bit of occasional thruster support. We have no way of knowing right now, of course, if it *has* controlling thrusters."

"Okay, definitely not a typical satellite, or a space station. So, what the heck is it?"

"We've got a call in to him to find out. But he never answers our queries directly if you remember. He usually makes a statement to the press when he does something that catches our attention. We expect him to do that again, shortly."

"Margaret, surely you and your *expert* analysts have a suspicion or two. Now, *again*, what is this thing?"

Margaret paused for a long moment. Then she cleared her throat, and replied with a slight waver in her voice, "We think it could be a space sunshade, or space umbrella. Or at least the start of one, anyway."

"And what would *that* be used for?"

"If you could build one big enough, perhaps in the order of a mind-boggling thousand kilometres a side, you might reduce the incident sunlight on the Earth's surface by a few percent or more."

"So, he's become a *terrorist*?" Bertrand barked with horror. "He's going to try to *blackmail* us, or something?"

"No, that does not fit his persona, thankfully, Bert," Margaret replied calmly. "More likely, we think he sincerely wants to do his bit to arrest or even reverse climate change, while enhancing his brand. It sure looks like he's built an effective sunshade, albeit right now a puny and rather insignificant one.

"The square object does not look black, like the back of a mirror or a solid object would appear from our vantage point on the Earth. Rather, it seems to be made of a material that lets no more than, say, ten percent of the rays from the Sun reach us through the screen, or rather reach the tiny, moving, square, shadow-spot on the rotating surface of the Earth. The screen might scatter light through random refraction, rather than reflect it back towards the Sun. That would be desirable, as it would reduce the effect of light pressure, and thereby reduce the thruster-fuel consumption that would be required to hold the object stationary and properly oriented in space. Of course, to stay at L1, you would also need some periodic thruster support to offset the varying gravitational forces exerted by other, moving, relatively nearby, massive celestial bodies, especially our Moon."

"Light exerts a pressure, is that what you said? How can that be?"

"Yes, it does, and its effects are most pronounced in a vacuum, like that found in space. Perhaps you might remember a science-class device in school that proved the phenomenon? The device was inside a clear glass vacuum tube like a light bulb. There were four small panels mounted on four symmetrical stiff wire arms, forming a wheel of sorts, all balanced on a vertical needle point. There was reflective silver paint on one side of each panel, and flat black paint on the other side. Photons are absorbed by the black paint, which replicates a so-called radiation absorbing black body, and photons reflect off the shiny side. The reflecting photons exert a force through momentum transfer. So, the otherwise balanced wheel spins in strong light due to the resulting unbalanced forces on the panels and no air resistance. You see, you can demonstrate that photons are both mass and wave energy, quantum physics you know, and…" She trailed off as she watched Bert's face quickly morph into a grimace.

Bert shook his head, then his face morphed again into a smile, and he replied, "Nope, sorry, not my forte, Margaret, that science stuff. Always feels like magic to me.

"But back on topic, by necessity. You all received the agenda. We've got *lots* of other things to talk about today. So, to *close* Margaret, Tim's got some kind of new technology, then?"

"Probably a *lot* of new technology, Bert. We know his corporation, PlastikTekhnologia, is doing a lot of research and development with carbon fibres, composites, and thermoplastics, mostly at his Earth-orbit space station. Zero gravity apparently can help in many ways with that kind of hi-tech stuff."

"So, this thing at L1 has a money-making angle then, or it's a marketing ploy, maybe? Perhaps he wants to demonstrate something new, in an ostentatious, showy kind of way?"

"Possibly, Bert. Or again, he's probably sincerely intent on making a sunshade. He'll need some big pocket partners to complete that though. I'm thinking about many other oligarchs, and wealthy advanced nations like us, no doubt."

"So, he's an oligarch that's altruistic. Bit of a strange cat, then?"

"Most would say so, Bert, but not everyone. He's very active in the global anthroposophical movement. He's been promoting and demonstrating the merits of a vegan diet and biodynamic farming for decades. And he went to a Waldorf school in Moscow. You know, or maybe you don't know, that such a private school uses the method of teaching started by Rudolf Steiner in 1919. It features experiential learning, tailored to a child's physical, mental and spiritual stage of development, and strives to fully develop the soul, apparently. Steiner was an Austrian philosopher, social reformer and esotericist… a possessor of deep, secret knowledge, according to the movement."

"Sounds a bit like the Wizard of Oz to me. I don't know whether that interests me or bores the hell out of me. Either way, the further exploration of what makes one Timofey Semenov tick will have to wait for another day.

"Again, we're pressed for time, even though I just encouraged you to run on. My bad! But one last thought. Is Timofey doing anything illegal? Aren't there space laws that govern these sorts of things?"

"There are, but they have not kept up with new technology very well. And a fully functional UN was needed for drafting treaties and getting nations to sign on to those treaties. Frankly, we haven't helped matters by basically de-funding the UN. We know President Winslow is trying to turn that around, but Congress keeps putting up roadblocks.

"Now, everything launched into space to ALINA-1 was done under the Russian flag and therefore it was all legal. But, for example, the rules governing geostationary orbit point-in-space allocations are technically still in place, but there have been numerous violations, especially by China, and the UN has been powerless or reluctant to do anything about it. Executing a treaty is one thing, enforcing it is another. And no one else it seems has being paying attention to activities at $L1$. It's been kind of the wild west out there."

"Thanks, Margaret. Please keep paying close attention and keep us posted. Okay, who's next… Phillip? So, what's at the top of the FBI's list today that we should know something about?"

2

PRESS RELEASE:

MOSCOW, August 18, 2039 — PlastikTekhnologia Corporation, or PlasTekhKorp, announced today that it has successfully assembled *in situ* the first *solnechny zont* or solar umbrella at the gravitational null point between the Earth and the Sun, or a point in space also known as Lagrange Point One, or L1. The feat is especially remarkable because of the considerable logistical challenges involved. L1 is about one-and-a-half million kilometres from the Earth.

The structure has appropriately been named ZONT-1 and was built using proprietary and patented technology developed by PlasTekhKorp. The modular, composite, thermoplastic structural components of the screen's frame, and the equally space-transportable liquid, polymeric-composite feedstock used to produce the sunscreen material itself, were manufactured at the corporation's Earth-orbit space station, ALINA-1, which was named after the CEO's mother.

Earth-based optical sensors have subsequently verified that the solar umbrella effectively prevents ninety-one percent of incident solar radiation from reaching the Earth. These optical sensors have also verified that the ion thrusters mounted in the solar umbrella frame are precisely maintaining the structure at L1.

CEO and Chairman Timofey Semenov commented, "We are elated that we have used our own ingenuity and resources to pull off this awesome feat. We have proven to the world that a practical and economic solar umbrella is conceptually feasible. Super-computer modelling suggests that if it can be significantly scaled-up to reduce, say, two percent of the solar radiation reaching the Earth, climate change could be arrested, or even reversed. The immense scale of such an undertaking is obviously far beyond PlasTekhKorp's capability, and we welcome discussions with other hi-tech corporations, and hopefully the most technically advanced and the wealthiest of nations, that might be interested in partnering with us."

About PlastikTekhnologia Corporation:

PlasTekhKorp is the nineteenth largest publicly owned corporation in the world in terms of assets, and EBITDA, or earnings before interest, taxes, depreciation, and amortization. Its primary business is the production of carbon fibre and thermoplastic feedstocks, and manufactured components and sub-assemblies, for the aerospace, renewable energy, automotive and transportation industries. It is also a major player in hydrogen production and distribution. Its research and development budgets are proportionally the largest of any corporation on the planet. One half of its common shares are held by its CEO and chairman, Timofey Semenov.

Timofey Semenov is completely transparent about his personal net annual income, which is only that of an upper-middle-class, Russian citizen. However, he diverts vast amounts of after-tax, dividend wealth, to supporting his Reverse Collectivization Foundation. This foundation works cooperatively with the Demeter certifying association of biodynamic farmers. Through hands-on training and the provision of low interest loans, it has enabled thousands of unhealthy and unhappy city dwellers to become healthy and happy biodynamic farmers, or modern day, prosperous *kulaks*.

Stalin considered *kulaks*, or independent, Russian, peasant farmers, 'blood-suckers' and hundreds of thousands of them died in forced labour camps during his Great Purge that occurred from 1936 to 1938. So, the foundation is effectively undoing a part of Stalin's destructive legacy. Collective farming in the Soviet Union was analogous in many ways to modern-day, worldwide, industrial farming, so the foundation's focus is moving beyond Russia.

Despite climate change, the foundation has transformed millions of hectares of what was once deemed 'wasteland' in Russia, Ukraine, and Eastern Europe, into the most fertile, self-sustaining farmland in the world. The foundation has sponsored and published several scientific studies that suggest climate change could be arrested and even reversed if the entire world converted to biodynamic farming. However, the uptake of this broader initiative by wealthy, industrialized nations has been frustratingly slow.

Semenov insists the work of the Reverse Collectivization Foundation will continue in parallel with the solar umbrella initiative. He believes that climate change must be combatted head-on for the survival of our species, and all forms of life on our planet.

3

Alain Dufort was the CEO of Wardenclyffe, the largest corporation in the world by any measure. He was also the wealthiest person in the world, and he was determined to stay that way.

Wardenclyffe had hundreds of divisions and subsidiaries, most of which were acquired through a long series of mergers and acquisitions. The corporation made virtually every conceivable electrical device and machine, from toothbrushes to bullet trains to super computers. Alain was an electrical engineer with an MBA, with a genius for recognizing new business opportunities, and knowing exactly how to extract the best return on investments. He held about twenty percent of the common, dividend-paying shares in the company.

He believed the mitigation of climate change could largely be achieved with vastly accelerated global electrification. He recognized the physical phenomenon of global warming as an ongoing catastrophe, but he could not overlook the convenient fact that it opened-up immense business opportunities for himself and his corporation.

Alain was ruthless and paid most of his front-line workers the least that he could get away with by law. And he dodged personal and corporate income taxes using every loophole that his crafty and shrewd, highly paid accountants and lawyers could identify.

With the most recent corporate name change, Alain wanted to tell the world that his next big move would be to follow in the footsteps of the great scientist and engineer, Nikolai Tesla. Tesla had built his Wardenclyffe tower to prove his belief that electrical energy could be directed and distributed over vast distances through the 'aether' and the Earth itself without the use of wires, and without having to believe in the existence of electrons. However, Tesla went bankrupt before he could complete the tower, which was the last item on his impressive 'bucket list' of accomplishments. He had died a pauper.

Alain Dufort would never have to worry about going broke in the manner that poor old Tesla had suffered. But he was as much a rogue and contrarian as Tesla had been. Alain had acquired lots of powerful enemies as a result of his strong-arm business tactics, and cold-hearted, manipulative business dealings. And all those many enemies would love to see him fail, for the first time in his life, and in a spectacular way.

Alain was fifty-three years old, an even two metres tall, with dark brown but greying curly hair, a ruddy complexion, and a handsome face. He ran three miles every morning before his breakfast, and he looked to be in his late thirties. He was married, but the relationship with his still beautiful wife had quickly descended into a loveless marriage of convenience. He gave his wife all the money and freedom she wanted, and in return, she politely ignored him. She knew he occasionally used the services of glamorous, highly priced and professionally discreet prostitutes, but she could not have cared less.

Alain's *raison d'etre* was to get wealthier and more powerful. He was an atheist, and he gave nothing to charity. He openly shared his last will and testament with the media. Everything would go to corporate shareholders as extraordinary dividends *if he died a natural death*. Otherwise, every penny of his estate would be spent by an executor foundation to ruin his many enemies, completely and ruthlessly, but legally.

Not surprisingly, Alain had no sincere friendships. But he was grudgingly respected by most government leaders and fellow capitalists and oligarchs.

The only platonic relationship Alain relished was with a Swiss lady, Emma Baumgartner. Emma had a PhD from Berlin Polytechnic in experimental physics. But her consulting firm engaged in industrial espionage. It sold its services to only the wealthiest of clients, and Alain was number one on its secret client list. Emma never revealed her sources of intelligence, and Alain never asked about them. But trusted private detectives had assured Alain that Emma employed a stable of highly intelligent, very attractive and engaging, bisexual, male and female agents, who made effective use of sexual encounters to dig up the good stuff.

Alain always met with Emma in an upscale Geneva bistro over lunch. They only met four or five times a year. If the weather was nice, they preferred an outside table. Emma insisted that they always arrive and leave separately. She wanted bystanders to think their encounters were strictly business, which they were of course, other than for the small talk.

But Alain found the small talk highly entertaining, as Emma Baumgarten knew a lot about virtually everything. And she loved to gossip about influential people, especially with a high-paying client who would conveniently and dependably pretend to forget the source of the information. Emma was sophisticated and cosmopolitan, and she was fluent in English, German, French and Italian. She always used English to converse with the otherwise French-speaking Alain, at his request.

Emma was thirty-eight years old, stunningly beautiful, with luscious and lustrous, dark brown hair that she kept on the short side. She was happily married to a wealthy, middle-aged Swiss banker who had many corporate clients… but not Alain Dufort.

Emma would only take physical gold for services rendered, and her husband's bank received the payments. And everything was above board from a tax perspective, with paper or electronic invoices and receipts.

And Emma only had to tell Alain once not to make a pass at her. She made it clear that there was a line that could never be crossed.

It was September 22, 2039 and a lovely warm day in Geneva, Switzerland. Such early autumn days were rare now in central Europe with the virtual cessation of the warm Gulf Stream current in the Atlantic Ocean. The demise of the current was the result of an ironic twist within the over-arching global warming phenomenon. The fresh meltwater from what was left of Greenland's glaciers effectively killed the siphon effect caused by salty, dense water falling by gravity into the extreme ocean depth south of Greenland.

Alain had reserved a corner table at noon in the outdoor patio of his favourite bistro. A three-metre high, vine-covered, stone wall surrounded the patio. The smartly uniformed waiters moved the neighbouring tables further away for him. There was no need for discussion. They knew who Alain was, and they knew his tips were extraordinary. Alain's four, plain-clothed, security people were seated at the two closest tables. One male-female couple looked to be foreign vacationers in their thirties. The other male couple looked to be young, local, possibly gay, body-building guys. No one looked out of place.

Alain sipped on chilled, sparkling, mineral water until Emma arrived. A freshly uncorked bottle of expensive Bordeaux red wine was positioned in the centre of the square table, which had place-settings for two. Alain only had to wait fifteen minutes for Emma to arrive.

"My, it's great to see you again, Emma!" Alain said cheerfully as he rose to greet her. She briefly smiled back at him and offered her hand to him over the table. They quickly shook hands and sat down facing each other.

"How are things with you, Alain?" Emma asked pleasantly as the head waiter suddenly appeared at the table to pour a glass of mineral water for her, and to top up Alain's glass. They both nodded with a smile when the well-groomed, well-mannered, immaculately uniformed, and middle-aged man also offered to pour some wine for them.

When the waiter had expertly poured the wine, and then departed out of earshot, Alain replied, still cheerfully, "My health is great and my businesses are great, but boringly so. And how are things with you, Emma?"

"I really enjoyed the summer, thank you, Alain. My husband and I had a marvellous time at San Tropez in July, despite the weird heat wave and prolonged drought. We had to leave a bit early, though, because of a wildfire threat. There's a smell of smoke in the air here too, have you noticed it?"

"I noticed it first thing this morning when I was out running, that's for sure. It took me half an hour indoors to cough it all out. Air-conditioned spaces have some advantages, I suppose."

"Yes, but I hate them with a passion. My sports are all outdoor types. And I love to go for long walks in wooded parks. Look, Alain, I'd like to run through some business matters with you before we start small talking and looking at menus. Then we can chat about whatever you like during lunch, and for a short while afterwards. Will that be all right with you?"

"Sure thing, Emma. The waiter won't come back until I wave for him. What have you got for me today?"

"Your people let me know, discreetly, that you were interested in ZONT-1. It's a pretty remarkable structure in space."

"Okay, that sounds good. Shoot."

"I'll start right in with some technical intelligence. The structural members of the umbrella frame are one-metre-a-side square in cross-section, and hollow tubular, with rounded edges. They are made from composite thermoplastic, with embedded carbon fibres and metallic conductors, using a sophisticated, proprietary, zero-gravity extrusion and continuous insertion process on ALINA-1. They are shipped by a dedicated shuttle spacecraft to the Lagrange One or L1 site in ten-metre-long sections, then pinned together by an attendant, robotic, service vehicle. Additionally, the robotic vehicle thermally bonds the joints together at the seams using a high-intensity laser-beam.

"The attendant service vehicle looks a bit like one of Arthur C. Clark's and Stanley Kubrick's pods in the classic movie *2001: A Space Odyssey*. It has a suite of multi-functional arms. It has a docking station for replenishing its ion thruster xenon fuel tanks. It positions the docking station in the shade behind the umbrella. It plugs itself into ZONT-1 to recharge its batteries. In addition, it has its own small bank of solar cells, and a plutonium-radiation-powered RTG or radiation thermal generator. It usually works without the need for remote human assistance from Earth, or from the astronauts on the ALINA-1 space station, using a long menu of pre-programmed routines, and with some sophisticated AI or artificial intelligence oversight for any tweaking required.

"There are tracks running down the inside of what is eventually made into a one-hundred metre-a-side square.

"Now for the really novel bit. To make the fabric of the umbrella *in situ*, another tubular bar traverses along the installed tracks from one side of the inner square formed by the structure right over to the opposite side. As it does so, it evenly excretes, like a weird sort of mechanical spider making a flat web, a liquid, polymeric-composite material. This material is held in place by surface tension, like a soap bubble, until it fully cures and hardens under the effects of ultra-violet radiation from the Sun.

"In a way, the fabric feed-stock material resembles the stuff dentists use for filling teeth, you know, when they direct a beam of UV light at the goop they squeeze into a drilled-out cavity. But this material is far different, and top secret. I've got people trying to figure out what it could be made from by working on the supply chain to the ALINA-1 space station. But it already looks like there are some deliberately placed, misdirecting red herrings to foil us. In other words, it will take us more time to resolve what this fantastic liquid goop is made of, and how it is made.

"The installed, fully cured, umbrella fabric works like a crude Fresnel lens. The solidified surface is both dimpled and wavy. It is translucent and does not reflect light. Rather it scatters light, and very effectively. Most of what shines on it from the Sun will never reach the Earth.

"The tubular, black body, or radiation-absorbing, structure surrounding and supporting the translucent umbrella is thermally stable. When the traversing bar is included in the calculation, it represents only about two point five percent of the projected planar area facing the Sun. But it will feel the effects of light pressure, all the same, and make station keeping at Lagrange Point 1, or the Earth-Sun gravitational null point, more problematic... but not impossibly so.

"Ion thrusters have been installed in the frame, fuelled by xenon, that is stored in tanks within the tubular members. Some solar cells are mounted on the outside of the umbrella frame on the Sun side. There are enough of them to meet the needs of the ion engines, with a bit of support from solid-state batteries. In addition, the batteries always keep an artificial intelligence controller alive and well.

"PlasTekhKorp has three geo-stationary satellites in Earth orbit. They have been positioned so at least two can always be seen at L1. They are referenced by the AI controller to manage station keeping, and to keep the planar surface always facing the Sun. The system uses precise triangulation algorithms and works a bit like the Earth-surface GPS system.

"At first glance, ZONT-1 can be readily expanded. A layperson might think, just connect another frame, and make another umbrella, right? Nope, station keeping will become more complicated and more difficult with bigger structures. There will be internal flexing within the grid that will distort the planar surface. Precise, coordinated, ion thruster bursts will be necessary to keep the surface flat and at right angles to the incident solar radiation, as well as keep the centre of the structure precisely at L1. Strain gauges have been imbedded in the structural members that can feed additional pertinent information to the AI controller. So, the AI controller and its ancillary telemetry apparatus will have to be upgraded and expanded as the structure is expanded.

"Ion engines create thrust by accelerating ions, or electrically charged atoms, using electricity. If you recall, as you *make* the devices, a neutral gas is ionized to produce a cloud of positive ions by stripping away electrons and storing them elsewhere for a while. The engines rely on electrostatics and the Coulomb force that exists along an electric field. After the positive ions accelerate through an electrostatic grid, a neutralizing device reinjects the stored electrons into the ion stream so it will disperse into space without interacting with the thruster.

"The reason I bring this up is that presence of a lot of ion engines make electrical grounding in space even more problematic. Most of ZONT-1 is made of dielectric or insulating materials. The electrical grounding is a multipoint scheme. There is a physical ground plane, or essentially a relatively big sheet of conductor, that is part of the structure. The inductance of this plane is very low, and lots of different electrical and electronic subsystems can be connected to it without causing an issue with noise between them, or heaven forbid, an actual and highly damaging electrical arc.

"Are you still with me? Is this too much information? I noticed you filled your wine glass again."

"No, that's all great stuff, Emma. Enough to earn your retainer fee, that's for sure. I think I would like to get in on this venture somehow, but Semenov hates my guts. The guy is holier-than-thou and lives in the clouds. He thinks his biodynamic farms are spiritually connected to the cosmos for fu... ah, sorry, for *gosh* sakes! Business is just a means to an end with him, and his end is a fundamentally changed world. We don't see eye to eye on anything, even though he is a big part of my supply chain. I'd buy him out or squeeze him out, but you told me before he'll never sell, and he'd rather destroy his trade secrets than see them go to me. And you told me before his key employees are fanatically devoted to him and will all quit if I take over the company.

"No, I'll need some leverage, a *lot* of leverage, to get anywhere with this noblest of charitable guys, some angle…" He trailed off as he took another prolonged sip of wine.

"Well, there may be something… something that might come about with a little help from Mother Nature," Emma mused as she stroked her chin. "You see, we think they may have overlooked something fundamental with their design. That's why I said so much about electrical grounding…"

"I'm all ears, Emma. But please, tell me over lunch, okay? I'm getting sloshed on an empty stomach."

4

Timofey Semenov had been waiting almost four months for a face-to-face meeting with Jorge Ramirez, the CEO and chairman of Mega Cloud Corporation. There were only a few gaps in their busy schedules, and overlaps were rare. Both men had cancelled set meetings twice because of unanticipated conflicting matters that had required their immediate attention. But at precisely fifteen hundred hours EST on January 6, 2040, Timofey was finally ushered into Jorge's palatial office in the top floor of a Manhattan skyscraper.

Timofey was forty-nine years old, average in height, physically fit, and quite obviously muscular from working out every day. He had a shaved, completely bald head, and Slavic features. He was wearing his standard English tweed sports jacket, high-collared white shirt without a tie, loose fitting black slacks, and comfortable, soft leather shoes.

Timofey had some Tatarian heritage, and he looked a bit like an out-of-place and out-of-time Mongolian warrior. He was the antithesis of an aggressive barbarian, however. He was a pacifist and a humanitarian. And he had never been married, but he had lived with three women during his adult life. No one would call him handsome, but many women had found him sexually attractive, and he was never boring. He had broken off each of his three serious relationships when the topic of children had come up.

Timofey liked not having heirs, as his entire estate was earmarked for his Reverse Collectivization Foundation. And he figured the world had far too many people anyway. Furthermore, he knew he could never be much of a father with the incredibly active, globe-trotting, and work-centred lifestyle that he enjoyed.

Jorge was of Mexican heritage, but he looked like a Spanish aristocrat or a matador. He was a young-looking forty-seven years old, tall, dark and handsome, as virtually everyone would agree. He never dressed casually. In fact, most of his clothes were made from the finest silk, like the stylish, light grey suit he was wearing today. He had been married twice, and he had a daughter from his first marriage, who lived with his ex-wife. He suspected his second wife was about to initiate a divorce, claiming correctly that Jorge spent far too little time with her.

In a practical sense, Jorge was married to his job, which he loved. Mega Cloud was the largest software company in the world, and Jorge was very effectively growing and continuously improving the corporation's already massive cloud technology, search engine, cybersecurity, artificial intelligence, tablet, smart phone and personal computer businesses. Jorge also owned Freeworld Press and offered free access to its globe-spanning news coverage with all Mega Cloud hardware and software purchases.

Jorge greeted Timofey at his office door with a firm handshake. "We have never met before, Mister Semenov, and I think that is a travesty," Jorge began with a smile. "Please, let's sit over here, in my little lounge area, on these deep, comfortable chairs."

Jorge had studied computer science at Stanford before he had completed his master's at the Harvard Business School. He had a cosmopolitan, American accent.

"Please, call me Tim. I would like this to be a friendly chat."

Timofey had studied mechanical engineering at Moscow Polytechnic University. He received his master's in economics from the University of London. He spoke excellent English with a slight British accent.

"Certainly, Tim. You can call me George if you would rather."

"No, I think I can manage the name Jorge. And it has a nice sound to it."

"Thank you, and I certainly think so, too!" Jorge laughed. "Can I pour you some coffee from this thermos jug? It's only a half-hour old. I like it black, but if you would like to add some…"

"No, black coffee is perfect, Jorge. And thanks very much."

"Great, here you go then, in a nice, plain vanilla, logo-free mug. I find I'm adverse to tacky merchandizing, right across our product spectrum. We can sip our coffee while we talk. And there's lots more left in the jug. So, this is not your first trip to New York, I imagine. Was this meeting all that brought you here, presumably from Moscow?"

"No, I had a few other matters to attend to, but I must admit, this was the one I was most excited about. I get to New York about once a year. I have, in fact, just arrived from Moscow, with a quick fuel stop in Gatwick. We have an Arrowhead II business jet."

"That is a marvellous machine. A blended wing body and hydrogen-fuelled turbofans. We have one too. First, can I compliment you on your spectacular ZONT-1 project? And how are you getting on with it these days?"

"Thank you. We are very proud of it. The space umbrella is holding station perfectly, and there has been no degradation of the refracting, diffusing and screening material. If you've been following the cynical and ignorant noises from my critics, there was groundless speculation the screen would quickly crack and fall apart under the constant ultra-violet light bombardment from the Sun. Our proprietary, composite, polymeric material will not cross-link and become brittle, and we knew that from extensive pre-trials at our ALINA-1 orbital factory. And the L1 facility has already survived two, albeit rather minor, solar flare episodes."

"So, you're not concerned about the CME that erupted a few hours ago?"

Timofey was caught off guard, but he did not show it. Instead, he smoothly replied, "As I said I just got off an airplane, Jorge, and I hate smart phones. You might see things differently, as I know you make the darn things, but I always suspect someone might be listening in or monitoring me, despite encryption. But you said a CME just happened... as in a coronal mass ejection?"

"Yes, and a big one apparently. They say it might be as bad as the Carrington Event of 1859, that is, if it heads directly towards Earth. And your space umbrella would be right in its path if that is the case. Electrical utility companies are taking steps to shut down or isolate parts of the electrical grid in some places in the northern hemisphere, and some communication companies are putting their Earth-orbiting satellites into standby mode."

"Ah, thanks for telling me all of that, Jorge. I'll get right on to it when we're finished. But you know, there's not much we can do about it at this point, anyway. Like other spacecraft, we shielded the key electronic components in ZONT-1 with metallic, conductive screens and installed multi-point grounding. It is what it is now, I guess they might say colloquially in America."

"Right, good, but most of those other spacecraft you just talked about were designed for operation in Earth orbit, well within the protecting magnetosphere. I just checked something out on the web. On the Sun side, where ZONT-1 is positioned, because of the bow shock effect from the prevailing solar wind, the protecting field only extends out about ten Earth radii, or out about sixty-four thousand kilometres. And you guys are out there about one-and-a-half *million* kilometres from the Earth!

"All those charged, highly-magnetized ions might cause one hell of an electro-magnetic pulse. I know from your second press release that you've got some solar cells on the structural members. And there are eight fully gimballed, electric powered ion engines with electric fuel pumps on pressurized, xenon-filled fuel tanks. And you've got *lots* of imbedded conductors in dielectric or insulating materials that could readily pick-up charge through induction.

"Is there any way you could rotate the structure to be perpendicular to the impending flare and ion stream, at least until it all passes safely by the facility?"

Tim now looked pale and worried. His mouth was suddenly dry, and the coffee was not helping him much. He stammered a bit when he replied, "No, it's an experimental, demonstration… a pilot project of sorts, to garner interest in expanding it into something big enough to do something appreciable… with regards to abating or reversing climate change."

Timofey poured himself another cup of coffee, smiled weakly, and added, "We'll just have to hope for the best, I guess, Jorge. Thankfully, there are no astronauts in harm's way. Everything to date has been done robotically, even the shuttle runs from ALINA-1 with supplies, xenon fuel and construction materials. And our robot tender out there should be all right. We send it behind the umbrella screen whenever the solar wind increases."

"Well, I'll hope for the best then, too, Timofey. I would love to be part of something that helps the world get out of this horrible mess it is in. In addition to climate change wrecking all our business models and cash flow projections, the ongoing human suffering it causes, and the decimation of virtually all other forms of life is staggering and heartbreaking. And still, with an obvious mass extinction event well underway, we have always had at least a third of the American population in total denial! The ignorance, prejudice and deliberate misinformation on social media is sickening! As you know, I'm part of the information technology supply chain and a key enabler of social media platforms. I'm a Catholic, and I pray for forgiveness. And in addition, of course, I pray for an end to endless wildfires, droughts, melting glaciers, a steadily rising sea level, failing ocean currents, floods, storms, pandemics... pestilence... and God only knows what else is coming!

"But I suspect climate change itself was not what you wanted to talk with me about today, Tim. Look, I blocked out another, let's see, twenty-five minutes or so for us. I'm truly sorry it cannot be more than that today."

"Thanks, Jorge, that's okay. Now, as it so happens, exploring your interest in a joint venture to expand the ZONT-1 structure *was* first on my two-item agenda. You have proactively highlighted a possible emerging threat for me just now. I should thank you for that, but frankly, you've got me a bit rattled. So, maybe we *should* delay the *real* ZONT-1 participation discussion for a while?"

"Yes, definitely. Let's talk about it again when we see how your facility out there weathers this solar storm... oh, sorry, please excuse the pun."

"Okay, no problem, Jorge. And I've heard similar responses from every other CEO I've talked to. You know, stuff like, 'please keep us posted', 'sure hope it keeps working', and 'best of luck'. So, there's been lots of interest in vast new supply chain businesses, but *no* interest in making the so-called 'charitable donations' needed to pay for it. The UN administration just arm waves, applauds the idea but sees no chance of getting nations, especially poorer nations, to help pay for it. I will need to get the G20 countries onboard, that's for sure, but I haven't figured out how to do that yet.

"But sure, let's move on, in the interest of time. My number two agenda item is both a money-making venture, and another initiative to combat global warming, mostly through carbon capture. The other nasty things it addresses include things like pollution, world hunger, poor nutrition, unemployment, topsoil depletion, land erosion, loss of spiritual connection to our world and to each other…"

"You want to talk about biodynamic farming, Tim," Jorge interjected. "I know you champion the idea. And I'm now the biggest holder of farmland in North America. Right?"

"Good one, Jorge, though I suppose that was not hard to guess. Would that be okay with you?"

"Sure. For your information, and it's no secret, I've been buying farmland simply because it has intrinsic value. I rent it out to industrial farmers. It's mostly prairie land in the increasingly arid US Midwest and Western Canada."

"Yes, I've heard all about that. And I have also heard that in many places, dustbowls are emerging again, especially in the Midwestern corn belts. Corn is an exceptionally heavy feeder, especially of nitrogen. Very few industrial farmers have been rotating crops with soil-enriching beans, alfalfa or clover. They just pour on the nitrogen fertilizer, which produces nitrous oxide, a greenhouse gas with three hundred times the warming potential of carbon dioxide."

"Before you go any further, Tim, I know of a study, an older one I guess, that said a total shift to organic farming in England and Wales would actually *increase* GHG emissions. The argument was with lower yields, more land would be needed to keep feeding everybody."

"Yes, I know about that older study, and others like it. They are all firmly stuck in my naysayers' arsenal of rocks to throw at me. The studies assumed that the benchmark industrial farming yields will stay steady as the climate changes further and soil degradation continues, which is blatantly false. I can show you *our* studies that prove as the fertility of the soil increases, self-sustaining, closed-loop, biodynamic farms get better yields than industrial farms. And the nutritional value and taste of the food produced is far superior."

"I wish I had time to read those studies, Tim. Now, in the interest of time, can you quickly run through the key aspects of organic farming, and this biodynamic farming method of yours?"

"Sure thing, Jorge. Certified organic farms don't use artificial fertilizers, herbicides or pesticides. They use compost and manure, and plant legumes, to strengthen the soil. As a result, they release less than half the amount of nitrous oxide into the atmosphere, and do not produce much in the way of groundwater and surface water contaminating nitrates.

"Biodynamic farms go far beyond typical organic farming. Half of our livestock feed must be grown *in situ*. At least ten percent of the farm acreage must be set aside for biodiversity, and a balanced predator-prey relationship. The farms also have more humus in their soils, and the soils sequester far more carbon as they are progressively enriched.

"For biodynamic certification, nine of what we call Steiner Preparations, made from herbs, mineral substances and animal manures, are applied using field sprays and blended compost. In addition, our cattle are grass-fed. They live longer than grain-fed cattle, so overall during their lives they spew out more methane, another extremely potent greenhouse gas that *still* leaks out of oil and gas industry facilities in a big way. But the carbon sequestration effect outweighs what methane our cattle produce. Combining all these measures with no-till farming methods, as much as possible, helps keep the carbon in the ground.

"Microbial biomass carbon is at least double on our foundation farms. The farms are as 'closed loop' as possible, and control pests and weeds on their own. Our philosophy contends that in time, with proper care the farm becomes a healthy, living organism, spiritually connected to the cosmos. We can't prove that, but we can prove our results.

"The spiritual and unconventional aspects that Steiner promoted do not appeal to all our farmers. For instance, some do not pay much attention to the lunar calendar or astrology for planting, etc. But they all recognize the sound agronomic system, and they become deeply attached to their farm and its place in nature. In other words, they don't want to leave after they get their farm up and running after several seasons.

"Our extremely healthy, sponge-like soils contend with floods and droughts better. Relatively speaking, plants tough it out very well on our farms in our changed and changing climate. And the pollinators like bees are in turn healthy too, and every farm needs those little guys for a healthy food supply.

"I could go into far more detail about our methods, but I'm conscious of the time, and I think I've gone over already."

"Thanks, Tim, that certainly helped a bit, and it perked up my interest significantly. Now, industrial farmers have effective lobby groups to retain both their supply chains and the markets for their crops. They will not roll over easily. But I'm fed up with helping to grow corn to make ethanol so it can be mixed with gasoline to appease special interest groups and politicians. The oil and gas lobby groups are also a pain in the butt. They keep getting governments to extend the deadlines for mandatory conversion to electric or hydrogen power in cars and trucks."

"Lobbyists and special interest groups did not roll over easily in Russia, Ukraine and Eastern Europe either, Jorge. But if you take deliberate, carefully planned, intelligent steps, amazing things can happen. Everyday consumers catch on quickly to superior food quality, taste and nutrition, and will pay a bit of a premium for it. We constrain our marketing of produced foodstuffs to twenty or so kilometres around a farm, to reduce the carbon intensity from transportation, refrigeration and packaging, and we use that in our marketing pitches. Our 'overall good of the planet' marketing angle is working better and better as things get worse and worse around us."

"Okay, Tim. Frankly, I'm not interested in selling you land, but I might rent some to you, mostly to observe first-hand what you say. And I don't want my wife to get my land holdings should we get divorced. Sorry, I'm thinking out loud, and that's probably too much information. But I think there might be a win-win scenario here for the two of us.

"So, say you, or your foundation rather, improves my land, and sets up some successful biodynamic farmers. Your foundation grows further in reputation and influencing power. And in turn, I have lots of happy, prosperous renters and sustainable, or better yet, increasing cash flow. The government gets to tax everybody. And we all help the planet. A truly reinforcing, causal loop. Sounds pretty good. Is that your pitch?"

"Right you are, Jorge!" Timofey replied with a laugh. "Spot on! The Reverse Collectivization Foundation would want to be able to pick through what land might be available in your overall inventory, though, so our demonstration project, or projects, will have the best chance of success. And if we believe we *are* successful, and we could prove that to you, we will hope that you might rent us a lot more land."

"Yes, that's understandable, about wanting to pick through our inventory, that is. So, why don't we do the classic, 'my people will now talk to your people' closing exchange?"

Timofey smiled, reached into the inside pocket of his sports jacket, and pulled out an envelope. He handed it to Jorge and said, "I was hoping you would say something like that, Jorge. Pertinent contact info is in there, as well as a couple of pamphlets about the foundation and what we do. And thanks so much for a bit of your valuable time today!"

They both stood up, shook hands, and Jorge said with a smile, "No, thank *you*, Tim, for initiating this informative little chat. We should do it again in a few months' time if our busy schedules allow. Now, let me walk you back to the elevator…"

5

Minutes after Timofey Semenov left the Mega Cloud office tower in Manhattan, he asked his limousine driver, personal aide and security guard, Igor Garin, to find a pay Wi-Fi kiosk. After about a twenty-five minute drive, Igor found a suitable one where he could park nearby. Timofey then asked Igor to use his own credit card to place a private direct phone call to the office of PlasTekhKorp's chief operating officer, Yevgeny Orlov. Igor had done this before for his boss and would simply claw back the phone charge on a business expense claim form. Timofey remained in the limousine while Igor worked in a kiosk stall. When Igor motioned that the connection had been made, they swapped places.

Yevgeny Orlov advised Timofey that, quite unfortunately, Earth surface and space-based sensors indicated that the bulk of the ionic mass and energy of the CME was headed directly towards the Earth, and therefore towards ZONT-1 as well. The expert consensus predicted it would initially arrive at L1 in about twenty-one hours. Yevgeny added that everything was still nominal at ZONT-1. The robot service vehicle, appropriately and affectionately named *Sluga Odin* or Servant One, was holding station about ten metres behind, or on the Earth-side of, the centre of the two-hundred-metre-per-side square umbrella. Therefore, it was also behind some intersecting, solar-radiation blocking, metre-wide structural members.

Timofey was pleased to hear that the corporation's executive ICC, or Incident Command Centre, was up and running in the PlasTekhKorp office tower. The forty-two-storey tower was just west of central Moscow. Timofey had picked the office tower location for several reasons. The Russian White House or parliament building was nearby to the north, just across the Moscow River. He and his executives made frequent visits there to lobby for their various initiatives and to stay in the government's good graces. The building was made internationally famous at the end of the USSR era when a tank fired shells into an upper floor with Boris Yeltsin standing nearby.

The PlasTekhKorp office tower was also close to the Kievsky Railway Station and a 'metro' or subway station. Railways and subways were the preferred modes of domestic travel for staff members and executives. Timofey's oldest sister and her husband, and their five grown children and their spouses, managed six biodynamic farms about five hundred kilometres west of Moscow's outer ring road. Timofey liked to make visits to the farms using the train system, and the farms were useful video backdrops for his public relations people.

Yevgeny then told Timofey that the international news media was hounding the company's public relations department for a statement, or better yet, a top executive interview or press conference. Timofey told Yevgeny to say nothing to the press for now, other than the CEO was on his way back to Moscow at the end of a routine business trip, the situation was nominal at ZONT-1, and conditions were expected to stay that way.

Timofey closed his telephone call by telling Yevgeny he would make his way directly to the ICC after his jet landed at Vnukovo Airport in Moscow. He confirmed Yevgeny would be their spokesperson, as always, if it was decided a press conference was the best way to go. Yevgeny had no problem with that. It was just another reminder that he was the heir-apparent of the CEO. He also looked the part of a calm, cool, and collected top executive, and he was a smooth talker who was quick thinking in front of a camera. Timofey added that Yevgeny's staff might as well book some slots in the big media centre in the nearby Slavyanskaya Hotel over the next few days. The hotel managers were fair about cancellation fees, as PlasTekhKorp was a big customer, and they would not blab to the press about the bookings.

6

What follows is the Freeworld Press translated transcript of PlasTekhKorp's televised press conference in Moscow. It began just after ten a.m. Moscow time on January 9, 2040. Russian news agencies insisted that the names and affiliations of their reporters be redacted. To eliminate speculation about who might have asked a particular question, Freeworld Press decided it would be best to redact all reporter names and affiliations.

"Hello, everyone. Glad you could make it on relatively short notice. For those of you who do not know me, I am Yevgeny Orlov, chief operating officer of PlastikTekhnologia Corporation. I will make a brief statement, and then I will take a few questions.

"As you are probably aware, a solar flare, and a massive solar coronal mass ejection, occurred about a week ago. Fast moving ions or electromagnetically charged particles made their way to Earth. The solar storm knocked out power in several places, most notably in Quebec, Canada; Minnesota, USA; and a few New England states in the USA. The high electrical resistance of igneous rock, like that found in the Canadian Shield that outcrops in northern North America, encourages geomagnetically induced currents to flow in power transmission lines above exposed rock.

"In terms of scale, the most recent solar storm was probably greater than the 1989 event, and smaller than the 1859 event. As in 1989, the entire Quebec electrical grid was blacked out, this time for almost ten hours. Electrical grids are remarkably resilient, but despite precautionary measures, rogue electrical current surges burned out some large transformers, circuit breakers, cell phone towers and substations. Also, a few Earth-orbiting satellites were temporarily disabled, and one may have been permanently damaged. However, our ALINA-1 orbital space-manufacturing facility, and our Lagrange-class, Earth-orbit-to-L1, robotic shuttle and transport spacecraft, were not damaged.

"The ion stream also seems to have passed by, or perhaps partially through, our ZONT-1 solar-umbrella demonstration facility. It is located about one-and-a-half million kilometres from the Earth, at the L1, or Lagrange One, gravitational null point between the Earth and the Sun. The fabric of the solar umbrella and its supporting structure appear to be intact, and our attending robotic service vehicle, *Sluga Odin*, is still fully operational. *Sluga Odin* has plugged itself in to the solar umbrella telemetry circuitry and is performing the same systematic and comprehensive diagnostic evaluation that it performed before the space-based umbrella was fully commissioned on August 18, 2039. In other words, *Sluga Odin* is behaving like a medical doctor, and is performing the equivalent of a thorough physical examination.

"Now, I can take a few of your questions. Yes?"

"How do you know the structure is intact?"

"We can see it from our vantage point on Earth with sensitive optical instruments, and *Sluga Odin* did a systematic, close-in fly-by before it plugged itself in to the structure. It gave us a video recording of the fly-by. Transmission time from L1 to the Earth is about five seconds. Because of the lag time, most of what *Sluga Odin* does is managed by its artificial intelligence controller. Most operations are pre-programmed, like inspection fly-bys and diagnostic checking."

"To follow up, are you saying there is no visual evidence of electrical arcing, or fires anywhere, either?

"That matter is still under review as we do further analysis. Yes, you're next, shoot."

"Is the space umbrella holding station at L1?"

"That too is still under review as well as we do further analysis."

"To follow up, if it's disabled, could it crash into the Earth, or other satellites, or is it more likely to fall into the Sun? And has this coronal mass ejection damaged the other scientific, data-gathering satellites at L1?"

"ZONT-1 is not going to move anywhere fast. We don't have anything to do with the three operational data-gathering satellites in the proximity of L1. We know where they are, or rather where their so-called 'halo orbits' are located, and we have been far enough away from them to avoid collisions. You'll have to talk to their owners about them. Yes, you have a question, sir?"

"I'd like you to answer the last question. Are the ion engines in the space umbrella working? And what about the space umbrella's artificial intelligence controller, is it working okay? And can you fix everything that's broken?"

"Let's let *Sluga Odin* tell us if something is broken when it's finished its comprehensive examination."

"But surely you must know if the structure is maintaining its position by itself! And I know the AI controller up there used to talk to you back on Earth without any help from *Sluga Odin*!"

"I didn't hear a question there. But if you claim to know something, why would you need to ask a question? Yes, you have a question, madam?"

"Could *Sluga Odin* help keep the space umbrella orientated the right way at L1 if some of the thrusters or the AI controller have been damaged?"

"That's a good question. Possibly, it's an amazing space vehicle. But it wasn't specifically designed for that kind of service. And I won't speculate about what might have been damaged."

"To follow up, don't you have to speculate about failures, and potential failures, to be able to prepare proper contingency plans?"

"Okay, that's a fair point. What I meant to say was I won't share any of our speculation with you folks. We'll just provide you with the facts when we have them. Yes?"

"When will you know all the facts then?"

"That would require speculation on my part." There was subsequent laughter in the room.

"I don't see the humour in that flippant response. Are we talking about a day, a week or a month?"

"Could be, or even longer. It depends on a lot of variables, some of which are not in our control. Yes, the tall fellow in the back row, your question?"

"Are you telling the Russian government what's really happening out there? And what do they think about all of this?"

"The Russian government receives regular updates of the facts when we know them, just like you do. You'll have to ask them directly what they think."

"Okay we will. So, to follow up, what does this do to your reputation and your brand? Can you build a bigger space umbrella after this?"

"We are an ethical, law-abiding, and tax-paying corporation that is welcome in one hundred and twenty-two countries. And we invent and employ the newest technologies to solve problems that no one else will tackle. That's our brand and I can assure you, it's intact. Okay, that's it for questions just now, unfortunately. I'm scheduled to check in with our Incident Command Centre again right now. Thank you. You folks have a nice day."

"Where's Semenov, the chief executive officer? What's he afraid of? How come we always get you?" A catcall followed this question.

"He never gives us a straight answer about anything, does he!" Another catcall.

7

From: Alain Dufort < CEO.wardenclyffe.com
Date: January 10, 2040
To: Timofey Semenov < CEO.plastekhkorp.com
c.c.:
Subject: We Know Exactly What Happened At ZONT-1
ATTENTION: PERSONAL AND CONFIDENTIAL

Timofey, I assure you the subject line is true. Please do not trash this email message before reading it completely through. I know we have had some rather feisty public exchanges in the past, and with sober hindsight, I for one sincerely regret all of those. The main reason I am writing to you today is that I believe there is a highly lucrative business joint venture that we could establish and profit from together that would also, and quite literally, save the world.

I will not reveal my sources. But to demonstrate the extensive breadth of our inside knowledge, here is a taste of it:

- ZONT-1 is unable to hold station or orientation on its own
- ZONT-1 is in a slowly decaying orbit around the Sun
- Electrical arcing has burned holes in the structure in ten places
- The umbrella screening fabric is intact with one trivial micrometeorite pinhole
- The AI controller has burned out
- Three of the eight ion thrusters have burned out
- One xenon tank is leaking
- *Sluga Odin* can slow the decaying orbit but not stop it

We first recognized this CME threat to the ZONT-1 facility over three months ago and we are quite advanced with top secret conceptual design changes and enhancements for a new and improved facility that one might choose to call ZONT-2. We see no reason to fundamentally change the basic structural design or the umbrella screening fabric. We applaud your excellent pioneering concept.

However, our solar cell, electrical, electronic, artificial intelligence controller, multi-point grounding system, Faraday-cage shielding, excessive-charge shedding system, and ion thruster design enhancements will allow ZONT-2 to survive another CME event, one as large as, or even larger than, the massive 1859 Carrington Event. And here is the kicker: *these design enhancements should also allow the project to ultimately pay for itself.*

When ZONT-2 is one-thousand kilometres per side, there will be twenty-five million square metres available for Sun-facing photoelectric cells on the vast grid of metre-wide structural members. If *all* the available Sun-facing area is covered with our high-efficiency photovoltaic cells, and with a generous allowance for the estimated *in situ* power consumption by the facility itself, we believe the net solar cell output would be at least three-hundred watts per square metre, which of course would be produced twenty-four hours per day, year-round. And we know how to send that immense amount of clean energy safely and efficiently to Earth. It would be the equivalent power output from over one thousand nine hundred of the largest nuclear power plants on the planet. That alone would go a long way to ending or even reversing our climate change crisis. As you know, China still derives over fifty percent of its electrical power from coal-burning thermal power plants.

You have never articulated in public how the immense capital and operating costs of a fully sized, climate improving, sun screening, space umbrella could be recovered. I suggest the only way is to tap wealthy nations for most of the capital investment, then share with them beamed electrical energy in kind, or give them a share of the revenue from selling such energy.

If we could meet face-to-face, in private, in a mutually agreeable place, and at a mutually convenient time, I will gladly elaborate on our concepts and re-design work. And if we get far enough along, we could also talk about a viable capitalization and revenue sharing scheme, *if you first sign the attached confidentiality agreement.*

I hope we can do business together, and for a very long time to come. I am greatly looking forward to your email response. Time is of the essence.

Cheers,
Alain

P.S. I think your COO Yevgeny Orlov did as well as anyone could have done at that awkward little press conference in Moscow yesterday.

P.P.S. My senior executives and I think he looks a lot like Boris Yeltsin, albeit a sober Boris, which was a rare occurrence as we understand it. Just saying.

8

PlasTekhKorp's COO, Yevgeny Orlov, lightly tapped a knuckle on the frosted glass window in the open door to CEO Timofey Semenov's office. "You wanted to see me, boss?" he asked quietly in Russian.

"Sure do, Yevgeny!" Timofey replied loudly, also in Russian, without taking his eyes off a computer screen that was positioned on a side desk. "Let me finish reading this draft email note, though. Come in and close the door. Oh, and pour yourself a cup of coffee from the samovar, and bring me a fresh cup too, thanks."

Yevgeny placed the two steaming cups of coffee in the middle of Timofey's ornately carved, wooden desk from the era of the last tsar. Then he sat down facing Timofey across the huge desk.

"Okay, it is set, Yevgeny," Timofey replied after a few more minutes of proofreading and two finger typing. He swivelled around in his chair to face back at Yevgeny, then dragged one of the coffee cups closer to himself.

Yevgeny then reached for the other cup, and asked, "So, that means you're going to meet with him?"

"Yes, over lunch, day after tomorrow, in Geneva, at what he calls his favourite bistro. Just me and him. He says not to worry, he will take care of *our* security."

"You are not buying that are you?"

"Not in the slightest. Igor and some of his security chums will be sitting nearby, and two GRU agents will also be somewhere close by. The GRU knows about this bistro. It seems Alain Dufort has always been a person of great interest to them. And they think they have a solid lead on who in our shop spilled the beans to his Wardenclyffe Corporation. I am anticipating that my main GRU contact will meet me in Vnukovo Airport just before I must get on the plane for Switzerland. His information should be illuminating, and probably distressing. Someone's head in our shop is going to roll, probably figuratively speaking, but one never knows in Russia."

"Okay, so you will want me to follow up in your absence?"

"Yes, but the GRU will handle the bulk of it. There will be an arrest. The President considers our secrets to be state secrets."

"Yes, I know. We are kind of a political crown jewel, or Fabergé egg, I suppose."

"Right. Do you still think I am making a big mistake meeting with Dufort?"

"No, after sleeping on it, I am with you now, completely. I agree we really have no choice, and there should be no harm in just talking to him, if we are wary of his tricks, and keep our eyes and ears open. The lawyers say his confidentiality agreement is a bit of a joke. There will be consequences if we infringe on a patent, of course, but our hands cannot be tied if we work in our own way with a new idea we hear about. There is more than one way to skin a Russian bear. And we hear lots of new ideas every day, from many sources."

"Okay, but Dufort is not a guy we want to cross if we can avoid it. If this progresses, the really binding documents will be the founding charter for a joint venture corporation, and the cost sharing and revenue sharing agreements between ourselves and government partners.

"And you know, Yevgeny, I cannot see how I could ever like the smell of this guy, but I might be able to hold my nose long enough to hear him out and turn something over to our negotiators. You would be the lead negotiator, Yevgeny, and I will not keep that a secret from him."

"Okay, no problem, Timofey. You know, they will have a lot of power at the negotiating table. They must believe they can somehow gather and disperse, or re-direct perhaps, the massive electrical charge picked up by induction from a coronal mass ejection. And there is a lot of hair on this, shall we say, 'beaming of energy to Earth for fun and profit' idea. They must be thinking of microwave transmission. If so, governments will want a lot of assurance that an energy beam can never stray and fry a city."

"Yes, I intend to press him pretty hard on that significant risk. And the other big poker chip he and his mega corporation bring to the table is influencing power, with governments and a vast international supply chain. His private intelligence gathering network is unequalled, and he is not afraid to use it. He has angered and hurt me before because he had somehow, quite mysteriously, gathered pertinent inside information, and therefore obtained the upper hand. And of course, he is a heartless, ruthless, selfish, son of a female dog.

"But between you and me, Yevgeny, we are probably going to need a partner like him to challenge and manipulate self-centred and or corrupt government leaders who will no doubt want many things in return for their capital investment and regulatory support. Our world is far from perfect, and neither is our country. Lots of smiling, innocent looking folks will have their hands out for kickbacks. Stating the obvious, if we cannot control and minimize corruption, ZONT-2 will fail. A very strong fist and shield will be needed on our side."

"Yes, I recognize all of that, too. But can I suggest that we structure any agreements with Dufort in such a way that we remain at arm's length? In other words, if dirty deeds must happen, he will agree to do them all, and in such a way that they will not come back to bite us?"

"My thoughts exactly, Yevgeny. Great minds *do* think alike. Oh, before we move on to another matter, what did you think of his Boris Yeltsin crack?"

Yevgeny laughed, and replied, "Oh, I have heard that one before, boss. And has anyone ever told you that you look like Yul Brynner?"

"No, who is that guy? And is that an insult, my cocky, brash and younger subordinate?"

"Definitely not an insult, my highly respected and venerable boss. He was a Russian-born guy, moved to America, successful actor, both in Hollywood and internationally, died in 1985. You should have a look at his photos on the web for a laugh."

"I will, thanks, I have not had many laughs recently. Now, about this latest so-called appropriation in China that borders on outright theft…"

9

It was January 17, 2040, and right in sync with the new climate-changed norm, a frigid and snowy, subarctic, winter day in Geneva.

Alain Dufort and Timofey Semenov had booked a closed-off, six-table, interior-area of Dufort's favourite bistro. Alain arrived about twenty minutes before noon with his four, security people. He was wearing a white polo shirt, casual black slacks, and a simple but well-tailored, black wool sports jacket. His plain-clothed security companions sat down in pairs at two of the tables in the room. Alain sat by himself at the corner-most table while they all waited. He noted that a bottle of cold, sparkling, mineral water and two blown-glass goblets had been placed in the centre of each table in the room.

Igor Garin and three of Timofey's security people arrived ten minutes before noon and sat down in pairs at two empty tables in the room. They were casually attired like Alain's people were, although perhaps not as fashionably. Two other black-suited gentlemen arrived five minutes later and sat down at the last available table, right by the door to the private room. Unbeknownst to Alain, they were plain-clothed GRU agents.

Timofey arrived exactly at noon and was escorted to Alain's table by an immaculately uniformed, elderly waiter. Timofey ignored everyone else in the room. He stood beside the chair positioned opposite Alain until the waiter had left the room and quietly closed the door behind himself. Then Timofey asked as politely as he could manage in English, "May I join you, Alain?"

Alain stood up, offered his hand across the table to Timofey, and replied amiably in English, "Of course you can, Timofey. In American-speak, I hope we can find a way to 'bury the hatchet', have a productive chat, and follow it up with a nice little lunch. What do you say?"

Timofey hesitated for an awkwardly long moment. Then he firmly shook Alain's hand, sat down, and said, "Well, I believe I can put aside our differences for a little while, or at least long enough to hear what you have to say."

"Good. Great. Can I assume that we are surrounded by our, ah, *friends* shall we say? And that we can both speak freely?"

"I think that is a good assumption. *Davai*, let's proceed."

"Okay. So, can I presume that you have signed the confidentiality agreement?"

Timofey pulled a neatly folded sheet of A4 paper from an inside pocket of his sports jacket and handed it across the table to Alain. Then he poured them each a goblet full of mineral water, while Alain unfolded the document, had a close look at it, smiled, and said, "Excellent. Off to a good start, then."

After taking a sip of water, Timofey responded with a blank face. Then he said rather severely, "Of course, I should tell you up front, Alain, that we are *most* disappointed that you stole information from us, and we wonder what value you actually attach to a confidentiality agreement."

"*Stole* is a rather harsh word, Timofey, is it not? It was actually *given* to us, and quite willingly."

"Yes, by our ex-deputy chief engineer, Fyodor Ivanovich Volkov. It seems he was seduced then blackmailed by an attractive young lady working for one Emma Baumgartner, who works within a long-term, rather open-ended contract with you. Fyodor Ivanovich has just been arrested by the GRU for selling secrets deemed critically important to the Russian state."

Alain sat quietly for a long moment. His face was now expressionless as well. Finally, he said with a touch of anger, "Very well done. I commend you for your insight, Timofey. Or should I commend your GRU friends?"

"The latter, I think. Two of their agents are sitting by the door. They're the guys in the rather tacky, out-of-style suits. They're harmless, unless provoked."

"Well, we certainly would not want to provoke them. So, I guess your underlying opening message is that when I do business with you, I'm also doing business with the Russian government?"

"No, my underlying message is that I am a pragmatic, private businessman, and I have to accept my personal reality, and the reality of a once great nation trying to recover its former respected status after two decades of struggle.

"I have managed to survive and thrive in a Russia laid low by a misguided, psychopathic, and evil former leader. If you recall, he figured invading the peaceful border country of Ukraine would be easy, and a critical step towards restoring the once mighty USSR, for which he held a rather perverted form of nostalgic love. Instead, his aggressive and criminal war-making ruined the economies of two great nations, killed thousands of Russian and Ukrainian soldiers and civilians, and forever traumatized the survivors.

"But to get back on point, modern day Russia allows me to run a for-profit business, if I pay taxes, and very discreetly but rather heavily grease a few palms. The country is *de facto* run by oligarchs, like me. We must all play by the rules of an old boys' club. But this constraint does not completely stifle innovation or ethical and gentleman-like behaviour."

"Okay, I think we can keep going then, Timofey. I know you are an ethical man, and a gentleman. And you think I am an unethical man, and a bit of a rogue, or even a cad. Frankly, I can be a gentleman when I want to be, and a complete prick when I don't. But we are both highly successful businessmen, who want to grow our businesses. And the only way we can do that is if this out-of-control climate change catastrophe can be arrested or better yet reversed. And even though you might find this next statement somewhat distasteful, catastrophes create opportunities for far thinking and risk-taking folks like us. So, would you agree that we are aligned with respect to wanting to end a catastrophe, while at the same time growing our businesses?"

"Yes."

Alain smiled, and said, "Good, let's build on that then. So, I think your ZONT-1 was a very good pilot project. It substantially proved some amazing new technology. And sadly, it encountered a threat that might not have been fully appreciated by even your smartest and most capable people."

"Yes, that's fair, and thank you. Now, Alain, you do not seem to have brought any supporting documents with you, or even a laptop computer to show me your concepts. So, can I presume that our discussion today will be high level and precursory?"

"Yes. But I think I can verbally expand on what I said in my first email note to you with enough clarity to take us to the next step."

"Okay. I'll listen then, carefully."

"That's great." Alain paused to take a sip of water. Then he said in a relaxed and confident manner, "First, I believe it is naïve to think wealthy, developed countries will agree to capitalize what we might eventually agree to call ZONT-2 without substantial economic incentives. I'm not talking about some kickbacks to a few corrupt leaders, although that might have to happen to some degree. I'm talking about sharing in a really significant revenue stream."

"This is what's driving your idea of beaming power to Earth-based receiving stations, and then into existing power grids. And how would you do the energy beaming part, safely and reliably?"

"Okay, it will require some significant re-design. For one thing, we will need to reconfigure the power and telemetry conductors imbedded in the structural members that support the screening fabric of the umbrella, and re-design those same structural members to allow us to add some sophisticated, hi-tech, internal, and external embellishments.

"We believe we can build an effective charge-gathering array that will be attached to the backside, or Earth-facing side, of the grid-like structural members. The array will be made mostly of metal. In an ion storm, it will attract, gather and direct electrical charge to sophisticated banks of capacitors. They will be located within the hollow structural members, and they will be isolated by Faraday cages. In fact, extensive use of our proprietary Faraday cages will be used throughout the structure to protect *all* electrical devices. Everything will be tied together, including the multipoint electrical grounding system. Dedicated AI controllers, separate from the station-holding AI controllers, will make it all work reliably.

"When sufficient charge builds up, it will be discharged to a bank of our proprietary masers. They will be attached to the front-side or Sun-facing side of the structure and will fire through apertures in the solar cell banks. The masers…"

"Excuse me, Alain, but what is a maser?"

"Oh, sorry, Timofey. Maser is an acronym. In the past it has meant microwave amplification by stimulated emission of radiation. 'Molecular' might be a better word than microwave for the masers we are proposing to use on the Sun side, as they will operate in either radio, microwave or infrared frequencies, depending upon what the AI controller thinks is best for efficient charge dispersion. The devices generate coherent radiation in the form of a beam, not unlike a laser, which operates in the visible light frequency range."

"Okay, so presumably, one would probably not want to stand in the way of one of those masers?"

"No, definitely not. The masers will ultimately dissipate the accumulated charge picked up in the structure from a solar flare or CME. The energy will be directed back towards the Sun, where it originated. It will be beamed in pulses, as the capacitor banks discharge, as frequently as required.

"Now, to make effective and commercial use of the surplus, steady-state electricity generated by the solar cell banks, we will use masers again, only just microwave frequency masers this time, positioned on the Earth-facing side. Electromagnetic energy will be beamed to relay receivers, and ultimately make its way to terminal, Earth-based receivers, where it will be converted to electricity that will flow into the conventional power grid. The intermediate relay receivers could be on the Moon, or on geostationary satellites, or both."

"So, this will be the aspect that will most concern governments and special interest groups. I take it a beam that strays from an Earth-surface receiver location would put living creatures at great risk, including human beings?"

"Yes, very true. The construction of ZONT-2 will occur over many years, however, and we will be able to progressively demonstrate the safety and reliability of the integrated energy transmission system to alleviate lingering concerns. And the terminal, Earth-based receivers will be in deserts, away from population centres."

"But we might want to start out by directing what you called our surplus, steady-state energy to the sterile and lifeless surface of the Moon as a safe demonstration of reliability?"

"You have a point there, Timofey. That might be a good fallback position we can use in negotiations."

"The other aspect that will greatly concern governments, Alain, is the immense capital cost of the facility. Unfortunately, not all governments share our sense of urgency to proactively combat climate change head-on. For instance, Russia and OPEC will not readily abandon oil and gas production. My hydrogen business is getting nowhere in those places. And frankly, my plastic and composite businesses depend upon the continuation of the petrochemical industry that uses crude oil and natural gas liquids for feedstocks. And so will ZONT-2 for that matter. And China has made noises for three decades about shutting down its coal-fired thermal electric plants, but it just keeps building new ones."

"Right, good points. So, we'll have to be very mindful of costs, and not be too critical of the oil and gas industry, and I guess China as well for a while longer. But no doubt others will keep up the attack on carbon-intensive industries, and I think we can foresee higher and not lower oil and gas prices, and continued coal production.

"But *we* should only use non-polluting liquid hydrogen and liquid oxygen to fuel the rockets we hire to move our construction materials into space. I suggest we will want to start off with, and maintain, a clean-and-green brand image to promote our efforts. I know you won't object to that over-arching strategy since you have a huge hydrogen business, and you are the father, so to speak, of ZONT-1.

"And I know you only used Russian launch vehicles for helping to build ZONT-1, and before that, for helping to build and now supply your ALINA-1 manufacturing satellite. Now, I acquired two surface-to-orbit launch companies that make use of reusable primary rocket stages. I still have them competing against each other to further drive down payload costs through innovation, focused supply chain management, and tight monetary controls. I'm pleased to say the strategy is working. From a global perspective, the companies are number one and number two in terms of cost efficiency.

"Another target area for cost reduction is the ion thrusters. Our improved conceptual design uses thrusters fuelled by either bismuth or iodine. Xenon is in short supply globally and therefore it is expensive. In addition, our thrusters will be bigger, and we will need fewer of them.

They will not be partially flush-mounted as in ZONT-1. Rather they will be externally mounted, temporarily so on the outside edges, since hopefully the overall area of the umbrella will be continuously expanded. The ion thrusters will be permanently mounted on both the Earth-facing and Sun-facing sides. If zero degrees is deemed a right angle to the structural element a thruster is mounted upon, that thruster can also rotate on AI command from zero to sixty degrees on a pair of gimbals."

"Okay, the thruster re-design sounds very interesting. And I intimately know all about the launch cost issue, and I can see why you would want to promote your own rocket-launching businesses. But virtually all wealthy, developed nations have Earth-to-orbit launch vehicle companies, some of which are nationalized. Can I suggest we would have to be ready during negotiations with a fallback position to allow those companies to compete for our services?"

"Yes, another good point, Timofey. Now, we believe your robotic *Sluga Odin* is an excellent design, and performs admirably, but we will need many more of them in uprated versions. And we think your robotic, Lagrange-class, shuttle or Earth-to-L1, transport spacecraft, could be improved upon, with a bigger payload capacity. And the rate of *in situ* assembly at the L1 construction site will be directly proportional to the number of supply shuttles and *Sluga*-type servant vehicles we have."

"Yes, and it will also be proportional to how many ALINA-type manufacturing facilities we have. And we do not yet know if we could produce the structural members you are talking about, with all the changes to mass distribution, bending stresses, imbedded conductors, additional fixation points and apertures for the significant external and internal embellishments you propose."

"No, that's very true. This takes us to where I thought we ideally would get to today. It's clear to me that we need to form a joint venture corporation. We could operate it on the high-level premise that Wardenclyffe and its supply chain would provide everything electrical and metallic. And PlasTekhKorp and its supply chain would provide everything else. We both would second experts to the JV corporation who would work in a coordinated fashion to design, build and operate a completely integrated, fully functional, safe and reliable ZONT-2. And you and I would handle the arguably more difficult bit... selling the idea to nations that we need onboard for capital investment, regulatory approvals, and perhaps, although this is uncertain and probably dynamic, international legal authority to operate our space-based, energy-producing and sun-screening facility."

"I agree with all of that in principle, Alain. However, may I suggest another negotiating chip that we may have to play? We might need to expand our Earth-based manufacturing facilities into nations where we do not presently operate. And promise those nations local employment, and tax revenue. And probably help them to enhance their electrical grids to be able to receive our energy in kind."

"Yes, that's all true too, Timofey. And it might take a lot more than that to win over some nations. I'm talking about tactics and methods that you might find profane or at least distasteful."

"Yes, I agree, Alain, it might require something like that too. Would you be willing to handle that component, and keep me and PlasTekhKorp completely out of it?"

"Yes, sure, no problem, Timofey. I would want full control of that potentially underhanded stuff anyway."

Both men paused to take prolonged sips of water. Then Alain asked, "So, Timofey, do we have at least the nucleus of a deal, or perhaps a preliminary, 'meeting of the minds' that can form the basis of comprehensive negotiations?"

Timofey smiled, and said, "Yes, Alain, surprisingly, I think we do. And you should know upfront that I will be asking my COO, Yevgeny Orlov, to spearhead negotiations from our side."

"Okay, we probably both will choose to negotiate through buffers. Say, is Yevgeny the guy in your shop who looks like Boris Yeltsin?"

"That's the guy. And he thinks I look like Yul Brynner."

Alain laughed, then said, "He's right about that, Timofey. Must be a shrewd fellow who also knows his classic movie history. I'll have to start thinking about the composition of my negotiating team. Frankly, I didn't think we would get this far today. But I'm glad we did, and I feel like we have cleared away some of the bad vibes between us."

"I agree. Should we ask the waiter to pass out menus to everyone now?"

"Yes, let's do that, Timofey. And should we include a wine menu?"

"Sure, Alain, and if we ever get a proper deal signed, perhaps we'll toast each other with Russian vodka?"

"That's a deal, Timofey."

10

PRESS RELEASE:

MOSCOW, January 26, 2040 — PlastikTekhnologia Corporation announced today that it has initiated discussions to form a joint venture corporation with Wardenclyffe Corporation. If consummated, the new corporate entity would re-design, promote, fund, sanction, construct and operate what might one day be called the ZONT-2 space facility.

PlasTekhKorp also confirmed today that ZONT-1, its demonstration solar umbrella facility at Lagrange Point One (L1), or the gravitational null point between the Earth and the Sun, was irreparably damaged by the recent, massive, Coronal Mass Ejection (CME) event. This same CME event is thought to have also caused at least one billion US dollars' worth of damage to electrical transmission equipment on the Earth, mostly in the province of Quebec, Canada. According to US authorities, it may have also disabled a Chinese military observation and communications satellite in near-Earth polar orbit. However, the Chinese government refuses to corroborate that suspicion. The US authorities also believe the Chinese satellite is in a rapidly decaying orbit and will soon crash somewhere to Earth. It is unknown if it contains radioactive substances.

CEO and chairman Timofey Semenov commented, "We are greatly disappointed that we have lost ZONT-1, but we have also captured many learnings from this massive, pioneering effort. We have also ensured the structure will never present any danger to anyone or anything. With instructions and assistance from our Earth-based and ALINA-1 engineers, the robotic support craft *Sluga Odin* has helped to give the completely disabled structure one big, final push towards the Sun.

"After extensive diagnostic checking, four ion engines were found to be working nominally. Thankfully, the four engines were equidistance from the centroid of the square, planar surface. Small back-up gyros connected to the thruster gimbal motors were powered up to maintain the structure's spatial orientation while the ion engines were producing thrust, albeit in a crude manner. Also, a way was found to bypass some burned out AI circuitry to simultaneously fire the engines. The engines burned up the xenon fuel in the tanks they could access until all the fuel was fully consumed.

"The result was by no means a perfect velocity vector, but it will do the job satisfactorily. The structure will take years to reach the Sun, but it also might be captured by the gravity wells around Venus or Mercury, and if so, it could fall into one of those lifeless celestial bodies. Either way, it now poses no danger to other spacecraft, human beings, or animal life.

"*Sluga Odin* has subsequently returned to L1 where it can hold station for years.

"We believe a partnership with Wardenclyffe, the largest and arguably the most technically capable corporation in the world, could help us build a better, more resilient, completely safe and reliable, solar umbrella at L1, one that could be expanded in stages to proactively combat climate change. It is early days in our discussions with Wardenclyffe, but so far no serious obstacles have been encountered."

Wardenclyffe CEO and chairman Alain Dufort also commented, "Our hearts go out to the many fine scientists, engineers, technicians and highly skilled workers at PlasTekhKorp. They put everything they had into the ZONT-1 project, and it had many successes. We are also hopeful we can strike a partnership arrangement with PlasTekhKorp that will allow this fantastic, new-and-improved, critically important project to move forward, possibly under the name of ZONT-2. Wardenclyffe also has many fine scientists, engineers, technicians, and highly skilled workers who are most certainly up to the challenge. We know from vast experience that synergy allows one plus one to equal at least seven."

PlasTekhKorp's share price fell by 9% when the disappointing news about ZONT-1 was first released, but the share price has since mostly recovered.

11

The US President's National Security Advisor, Bertrand Latimore, hurriedly sat down opposite the Vice President of the United States, Christos Balaskas. Christos was sitting in his office in the White House behind a busy-looking desk. The Vice President preferred to be addressed as Chris in informal situations.

"Thanks for swinging by, Bert." Christos opened the conversation cheerily, displaying his typical outward calm. He was in fact stressed out, but with lots of practice, he was proficient at hiding his true emotional state. He added, "Just looking for an update on this ZONT-2 development, and anything else that's on your mind. As you know, I'll be filling in for the President while she's making her hugely significant and very busy European tour with a good chunk of the Cabinet. You know, I'm talking about the meetings with the G7 countries in London, the British PM and his cabinet, the NATO Parliamentary Assembly, and formal state visits to three EU leaders."

Christos was thirty-nine years old, openly gay and married for ten years to the most highly regarded neurosurgeon in Maryland. Bertrand had been homophobic until he had got to know Christos. He now considered Christos as the most capable person in any government position. Bertrand viewed him as brilliant, affable, empathic, tolerant and respectful to everyone he met.

Christos was also tough when he was under attack by political opponents, but almost in a motherly sort of way. He had the innate ability to make most people, including ultra-conservative media people, or more importantly their followers, feel guilty for saying hurtful and destructive things. He did this without resorting to retaliatory verbal abuse and personal attacks. Bertrand thought he would make a fantastic President, but he also thought the USA was still not ready for an openly gay President.

"I didn't bring any notes with me, Chris, but I think I can effectively shoot from the hip on this one for you," Bertrand replied while wiping his brow with a folded handkerchief. He was unaware that he was now doing that routinely when he met with his staff, peers and superiors.

"Sorry, I should have warned you, Bert, about the main topic. I've just been so darn busy trying to get ready to fill in for Kate. Please, just do your best, that's all I can ask."

"Okay, here goes. The negotiations between Wardenclyffe and PlastikTekhnologia are continuing. Rumour is they are dealing with the minutiae now, which sounds encouraging. But both parties are refusing to talk to the press about where they're at. The wild speculation in the rumour mill is making their stock prices swing up and down dramatically. This volatility would probably concern most corporations, but not these two. They seem to be remarkably aligned on making this happen, and outwardly oblivious to the incredible, increasing noise around them.

"On the homeland security front, our right-wing foes have been promoting fake news on every social media platform about a Chinese conspiracy to destroy the free world. They claim ZONT-2 will be secretly controlled by the Chinese, who will block out all sunlight to some places, and destroy other places with microwave beams. And farmer lobby groups are expressing concern about disproportionately getting too much shade and not enough sunlight, even though they support fighting climate change in principle. And a pro-family lobby group is worried periods of sudden darkness during the daytime will cause motor vehicle accidents, putting children in school buses especially at risk. This notion or phobia is starting to take off in many irrational and unsubstantiated directions on social media platforms. And some unions have latched on to it too, citing concerns about worker safety during what they are calling, 'artificial total solar eclipses'. So, the now normal, fringe group misinformation campaign is well underway in the USA.

"The Chinese government has responded in typical fashion using the classic projection tactic employed by a past, one-term, US president who I won't have to name. They are accusing the West of a conspiracy to destroy China with ZONT-2.

"The CIA believes the inner circle of Chinese communist leaders were caught with their pants down. They didn't think ZONT-1 would work as well as it did, nor did they think a mega corporation like Wardenclyffe would be interested in a partnership deal to rescue the project. The Chinese Communist Party is feeling populist pressure to build a competing, Chinese version of ZONT-2, even though that's a physical impossibility. There's only so much room in the good spot, or the null-gravity spot, between the Earth and the Sun. The CIA thinks they will try to use the UN, or what's left of it, and space law, for what that's worth, to stifle the ZONT-2 project, or at least to slow it down.

"The UN Director General, Chet Bunma, feeling the intensifying political heat from China, has said that the UN is now investigating whether PlastikTekhnologia Corporation violated UN Resolution forty-seven slash sixty-eight, which outlines principles relevant to the use of nuclear power sources in outer space. It seems the corporation's robotic tender craft, with the rather cute name of *Sluga Odin* is partially powered by a radioisotope generator that is fuelled by highly radioactive and highly toxic plutonium. PlasTekhKorp subsequently issued a press statement that claimed they followed the guidelines in the resolution to the letter. They say they can conclusively prove that until the plutonium left Earth orbit, it was protected by a containment system capable of withstanding the heat and aerodynamic forces of re-entry to the Earth's atmosphere. NASA and the CIA think they have a solid case, and the UN will likely just let this challenge die on the vine.

"The owners of the three working satellites in halo orbits around L1, or the former ZONT-1 location in space, have filed a class action, civil lawsuit in a US district court against PlasTekhKorp. The suit alleges the group has suffered commercial revenue losses, and allegedly irreplaceable scientific data losses, due to the quote, 'obstructive presence of the ZONT-1 structure'. They might have a point. The suit also seeks compensation for future losses should ZONT-2 proceed. Success with that tag-on element seems unlikely, as the damages are speculative and have not yet occurred. There might be a solution the two parties in the suit can agree to out of court. For instance, there is probably no significant technical reason why a few scientific sensors and optical instruments could not be installed on the ZONT-2 structure to restore the data stream. But this one will just have to play out.

"Various terrorist groups have expressed intense opposition to ZONT-2. For instance, the supposedly Islamic UPKP organization says, and I paraphrase, if climate change is happening, which it claims is doubtful, God meant for it to happen, and it would be an unforgivable sin to build a space umbrella to combat it. The CIA thinks some OPEC countries are secretly funding UPKP, and possibly another, emerging, and so far non-violent lobby group called, 'Friends of the Sun'. OPEC and other non-member oil producing nations would be the big losers if the world someday got all the energy it needed from a space-based solar cell facility. The coal industry would also face ruination, but demand for coal has significantly waned, other than from China.

"Rogue states like North Korea are starting to insist that the UN stops *all* enabling work on ZONT-2 until space laws are updated to properly deal with it. The CIA thinks this might just be a ploy by some dictators and oligarchs to extract more for themselves during negotiations, before ultimately agreeing to participate in the project. I'm leaning that way myself, but time will tell.

"The President will probably hear widespread support for the project in Europe, or at least general interest in it. We have withheld comment so far, but the UK, France, Germany, Japan, South Korea, Switzerland, Israel, Canada, Mexico, Australia and New Zealand have all said they are notionally behind it but need to see more details about it. Russia has also, perhaps surprisingly, stated its support for it in principle, which has probably alarmed or even angered the Chinese government. Russia has been affiliated with OPEC off and on for several decades, that is, when they have seen some advantage in a loose affiliation. They have a huge petrochemical industry now, and they probably think they can corner the market with exclusive deals to supply Russian-based PlasTekhKorp with what it needs for ZONT-2.

"The international green movement is firmly behind the whole scheme, and polls suggest young people around the world want to see it happen. As you know, our party is about to go public with support for it in principle.

"I guess that's about it, Chris. I may have forgotten a few things, and I'm sorry if that proves to be the case."

"No need for an apology, Bert, that was great. And the President *does* intend to express support in principle for the project at a press conference when she returns from Europe. Now, is there anything else I should know before Kate leaves?"

"Yes, a few things, Chris. Now, the World Health Organization is getting increasingly concerned about yet another emerging novel virus…"

12

JOINT PRESS RELEASE:

MOSCOW, March 17, 2040 — PlastikTekhnologia Corporation and Wardenclyffe Corporation are pleased to announce today that they have executed a Memorandum of Understanding to form a joint venture company that will design, promote, fund, sanction, construct and operate a Sun-orbiting space facility that they will call ZONT-2.

ZONT-2 will be an integrated solar-screening umbrella and solar-power generating facility. It will be located at the gravitational null-point between the Earth and the Sun, at a point in space also known as L1. It is believed that as this facility is expanded, it will progressively help to combat global climate change through a slight reduction of incident sunlight on the Earth. It is also believed that as the facility grows in stages it will increasingly displace carbon-intensive and polluting electrical power sources on the Earth.

The two companies are proposing to construct ZONT-2 in discrete phases, with defined milestones and accompanying decision gates. Certain criteria will have to be met before a subsequent construction phase can begin. These criteria will include a full evaluation and analysis of the facility with respect to its effect on climate change, and its safety, reliability and efficiency. As well, the incremental impacts on Earth-based life form activity will be fully evaluated and considered, such as the possible effects of a shadow spot as it traverses the Earth's rotating surface. It is thought that numerous mitigation measures are available to negate potential impacts, such as noting in local weather forecasts the time of day when the dimming of the sun will occur.

All relevant stakeholders will be consulted at each construction phase decision gate, and their views will be objectively considered and highly valued.

The pre-construction design and project sanction process also has three defined milestones with decision gates.

Phase One will combine the drafting and refinement of a comprehensive Basis of Design document, and in parallel, the promotion and interactive discussion of the evolving project with all relevant stakeholders. To pass through the first decision gate, a Memorandum of Understanding will have to be executed with enough countries to cover the capital costs of a defined Stage One of construction.

Phase Two will combine the formulation of a comprehensive Detailed Design document, and in parallel, the negotiation and drafting of capital funding and electrical power/revenue sharing agreements with partnering nations. The partnering nations will share the cost of a defined Stage One of construction. Ultimately, partnering nations will also share in the revenue stream, or actual power stream, from energy beamed to the surface of the Earth, in proportion to their capital contributions.

Phase Three will combine the negotiation and execution of binding agreements with all applicable regulatory authorities, and in parallel, the final sanctioning by the board of directors of the joint venture company, the Wardenclyffe Corporation, and the PlastikTekhnologia Corporation.

The joint venture company will be named ZONT-2 Corporation. It will be headquartered in Geneva, Switzerland, with a significant ancillary presence in Moscow, Russia and Austin, Texas, USA. Staffing of ZONT-2 Corporation has begun with secondments from the two parent companies. The recruitment of additional human resources will begin shortly. This marks the beginning of Phase One of the pre-construction process.

13

Nasir Abd Al-Rashid was an oil-production, refining and petrochemical industry oligarch. He owned swank and luxurious condos in all seven Arab states around the Persian Gulf. But his favourite place was Dubai in the United Arab Emirates. He went through the motions of being a practising Sunni Muslim. But he loved the luxurious decadence of Dubai, with its high-end shopping centres and restaurants, ultramodern architecture and wild nightlife. His perversions were many, and he enjoyed them all using a variety of cunning disguises.

Nasir was clean-shaven, but today he was sporting one of his many fake beards. He was also dressed as an Arab sheik. He had been waiting for twenty minutes at a corner table in a traditional, all-male coffeehouse in an out-of-the-way part of Dubai. The open air, fully roofed enclosure was virtually empty. When his companion arrived, Nasir noted the man was similarly garbed, and he was sporting a different beard than the last time they had met.

"Welcome, my friend," Nasir said quietly in Arabic. "God is great."

"Yes, truly, God is great," his companion replied in Arabic as he sat down and adjusted his robe. "And merciful too, we hope."

"Truly. Let us quietly enjoy some excellent coffee while we gather our thoughts in this most pleasant of places."

"Yes, let us do that."

Nasir's companion was Mustafa Faez, and he was the leader of the UPKP terrorist organization. Nasir knew Mustafa's devotion to the Sunni religion was as phony as his own. Mustafa had personally tortured and killed hundreds of people. But he was not sadistic. He used terror and violence to achieve an end. And his end was to be as rich as Nasir Ab Al-Rashid with all the many accompanying pleasures. Mustafa was a *de facto* mercenary general, and one of the finest in the business.

When they started drinking their second cups of coffee, Nasir broke the silence and said quietly, "The Chinese government has agreed to all of your demands, including your fees, and the supply of all the munitions and explosives you require. But you must never reveal their involvement in your activities, or my involvement either, for that matter."

"That is excellent, and of course, agreeable. You and the Chinese will keep the money, explosives and arms flowing, and our jointly owned secret will be safe forever. The UPKP will proceed under the blessed banner of saving the soul of Islam. The ZONT-2 project is blasphemy of the highest order, and a direct afront to God, and it must be stopped. Are you okay with that over-arching philosophy?"

"That is the philosophy I want, and what the Chinese government wants. Will you have any trouble recruiting suicide bombers?"

"Not in the slightest, with that glorious banner of the jihad held high above our heads."

"Okay, and have you assembled a prioritized list of targets?"

"Yes, it will all start in London, then move on to Brussels. Then we will hit Tel Aviv, and that one with the greatest enthusiasm, of course. Then we will hit Moscow, Geneva, Paris, New York, Frankfurt, Ottawa and Melbourne. We will add to the list of course as necessary, until the cause is won."

"That sounds appropriate. Do you have any more questions right now?"

"Yes, but only two. Why did you approach the UPKP, and not ISIS, or the Taliban, or Al-Qaeda, or…?"

"You are professional and not fanatical. The Chinese government deals with the Taliban while holding their noses to fix and maintain a supply of lithium, and rare earth minerals and metals, from Afghanistan. ISIS and Al-Qaeda and the rest march to their own drums, and their allegiance cannot be trusted."

"Okay. I understand. And lastly, how does OPEC fit into all of this?"

"They don't. I find their petty internal squabbles, indecisiveness and ineffectiveness as a cartel nauseating. The Chinese government is of the same mind. They have a personal arrangement with me that meets all their needs. Nothing on paper of course, just a handshake, but that's my preferred way of doing business anyway."

"Very well. Can we shake hands now to seal *our* deal?"

"Yes, my most capable friend. Let us do that. I will pass a word to you as always through your young chap as to where and when we should meet again, and again both of us must always be in disguise, of course."

"Amen. Here is my hand."

"Your hand is gladly accepted. And yes, amen."

14

NEWS FLASH:

London, UK, April 17, 2040, 14:35 GMT: Freeworld Press is reporting that there has been a powerful explosion just inside the main door of the famous Savoy Hotel in London. There have been at least three fatalities and twelve serious injuries because of the blast. One of the fatalities was the US Deputy Secretary of State, Mark Granger. The other two fatalities are believed to have been the on-duty doorman of the Savoy Hotel, and a US Marine sergeant. London's Metropolitan Police Service advises that their names cannot be released until close family members have been notified.

Freeworld Press reports that two eyewitnesses claim to have seen a young man wearing a backpack try to forcefully make his way past security at the hotel entranceway a few minutes before US President Kate Winslow was scheduled to depart for the G7 meeting in Kew Gardens, Richmond. It has been confirmed that the US President was not injured by the powerful blast.

The Middle East based terrorist organization UPKP is claiming responsibility for the blast on social media. They are saying this is the start of a holy jihad against the ZONT-2 space umbrella project.

NEWS FLASH:

Brussels, Belgium, April 22, 2040, 09:51 GMT: Freeworld Press is reporting that a terrorist attack has been foiled at the road entrance barricade outside NATO headquarters in Brussels where the NATO Summit is currently getting underway. Two assailants were shot dead before the high explosives in their two-and-a-half tonne truck could be detonated. The area has been fully secured and sealed off as forensic experts meticulously comb the scene for evidence.

The terrorist organization UPKP is claiming responsibility for the attack on social media. They are saying this is the second battle in the holy jihad against the ZONT-2 space umbrella project.

A NATO spokesperson said the NATO Summit is proceeding as scheduled, and all NATO heads of state are uninjured and attending the summit.

15

Timofey Semenov was frustrated. He had struggled while trying to perfectly type a series of long and complicated passwords into his personal computer. Then he had tried four times to perfectly enunciate a voice password into the microphone on his headset. And then he had rigidly posed for a series of face and retinal digital photographs. The software package seemed unhappy with a few of the images and insisted upon additional images. Finally, Timofey established a cybersecure videoconference link with Alain Dufort, and with Holt Carson, the president and CEO of the new joint venture company known as ZONT-2 Corporation.

The connection with Alain came up on Timofey's large computer screen first. Alain said cheerfully, "Hey, Tim, there you are at last! My, that certainly was an ordeal, wasn't it! Do you really think all of this cyber preamble is necessary?"

"Hello, Alain. My friend Jorge Ramirez with Mega Cloud assures me this is the best cybersecure link available. And yes, I think face-to-face meetings and travel are out for us for a while."

"Your friend? How did that come about?"

"He's leasing to my foundation considerable swathes of farmland in Saskatchewan, Minnesota, Illinois and Iowa. The foundation is establishing family, biodynamic farms on those acreages."

"Oh, right, that's the other thing you're passionate about, isn't it? Can't be much money in it that I can see."

"No, not for the foundation, or for me. But this is not really about the money. Some families will be a lot healthier and happier, and a bit better off financially. And the people that live around the farms will be enjoying more nutritious and tasty meats and vegetables. And it will do some good at combatting climate change."

"If you say so, Tim. Can't do as much good as ZONT-2 will though."

"It's more in the every-bit-counts camp, I agree, Alain, unfortunately. Although, as I've said publicly many times, if most of the world converted to biodynamic farming, we would not need something as fantastically expensive and challenging to design, sanction, fund and construct as ZONT-2."

"Can't see that happening, sorry, but that's just my cynical side talking. Just like I don't believe every person will completely give up their hydrocarbon burning machinery unless forced to do so. However, please, let me know every now and then how your special farming project is coming along. I like spectator sports."

"Will do, and gladly. Oh, it looks like Holt has just joined in. Hello, Holt! You are successfully connected with Timofey and Alain now."

"Howdy, y'all! I tell you what, boys, I'm sure glad this fancy software recognized my froggy voice. Got a bit of a head cold this morning, and it's raining in Austin for the first time in two months. Is it any better in Geneva and Moscow?"

Holt Carson was a Texan, a second-in-class West Point graduate, a civil engineer, and an early-retired US Army Brigadier General. He had received a University of Texas MBA a year after leaving the Army. He had been the overall project manager during the construction of several hi-tech NORAD military installations, including one in space. NORAD had recently switched most of its attention from Russia to China, but it was still very much alive.

"It's cold and clear in Moscow," Timofey replied.

"The sun is coming out in Geneva after a brief rain shower," Alain replied. "It's been dry and cold here. There is no sign of the spring flowers yet. You missed our preceding conversation, Holt, but I think Tim is right. We'll need to meet like this for a long while, unfortunately. The Swiss Federal Intelligence Service believes we are all high-priority targets of this dastardly UPKP group."

"The Russian GRU thinks the same thing," Timofey added with a bit of angst in his voice.

"So does the CIA," Holt growled angrily. "And I never thought I'd get a call from one of those spooky dudes."

"The GRU has been in very active discussions with the CIA, Mossad, and MI6," Timofey shared with the others. "I got that straight from my high-level GRU contact. There was not much left of the suicide bomber in London for forensic analysis. The two eyewitnesses both said he was a dark-skinned Caucasian, crazed or scared looking, and young, maybe early twenties.

"In Brussels, the forensic analyses of the NATO terrorists have been more successful. One attacker was a Saudi male, the other a Syrian, both unknown to police and intelligence agencies. The weapons in the truck were all Chinese made. The undetonated explosives were all types that the Chinese military likes to use, and they may have originated in China, or Vietnam, a close Chinese ally.

"So, the GRU suspects the Chinese government may be funding and or arming this UPKP group. They say they believe the CIA is actively chasing the possible money trails that could firmly establish such a link."

"Then the President's upcoming press conference should be rather interesting," offered Holt.

"I suspect President Kate Winslow will avoid saying anything about China without conclusive evidence of its involvement," Alain predicted. "But the head of the Swiss Federal Intelligence Service is a friend of mine, and he owes me a few favours. I think he and I should pay a personal visit to the Chinese Ambassador here, and just let him know we would prefer negotiating project participation deals with China rather than ducking bullets and bomb shards. Or something like that."

"Yes, I think we need to do something proactive along those lines, but tactfully of course, so we don't burn bridges before we get to them," Timofey replied. "The Chinese government is increasingly isolated in the world. They have fully nationalized all their companies again, from the biggest to the smallest. Russia and the Western countries have imposed long-standing sanctions and tariffs on them for detaining, arresting, unjustly convicting and even executing foreign nationals, starting with some Americans and Canadians over two decades ago. There are non-stop Chinese Air Force and Navy incursion incidents in and around the South China Sea. And there are rumours that the Chinese Communist Party is not pleased about the nation's steadily increasing trade imbalance, shrinking GDP and rising unemployment. Their top political leaders must be feeling intensifying dissatisfaction from the outer party, which might make them behave even more aggressively and irrationally."

"And we should keep a close watch on what China says and does in the UN General Assembly, and especially in the Security Council," suggested Holt. "And keep a close eye on what the G20 countries in particular think about that, through your government contacts. My government contacts are frankly limited in number, except with the US military, and the Canadian military people who I got to know within NORAD."

"To slightly change gears, the UN has officially dropped its investigation into the safety of the Earth-to-space method we used to deliver the radioactive decay, power generating plutonium we put into *Sluga Odin*," Timofey continued. "And we think we can settle the L1 satellite class action lawsuit out of court for a bit of money, and a promise to let the three parties that sued us put some scientific and commercial sensing instruments on ZONT-2. That one is for you to follow up on, Holt. And you owe us a formal progress report on the comprehensive Basis of Design document in a few days, I believe."

"Yes, we have not forgotten, and you'll both get the report on time," Holt responded confidently. "I think you'll both be pleased with it. We've already addressed the additional Sun and Earth looking scientific sensor issue, and it's not a problem.

"We are now fully staffed up and we have really beefed up our cybersecurity shields. I told the FBI there have been numerous attempts to hack into our document management system. I mentioned it also to the CIA guy who called me, and I mumbled to him that maybe the Chinese government was behind the attacks."

"It's critically important to know if that is the case, and right away, Holt," replied Alain forcefully. "We should all ask our intelligence agency contacts to investigate the cyber breach attempts or have the right government agency do it. I would like some more ready ammo when I meet with the Chinese Ambassador.

"Now, we had better spend the rest of our allotted time today coordinating our lobbying efforts, and upcoming meetings with G20 nations. We do not want to lose momentum. We must complete Phase One to beat out a ruthless and powerful competitor like the Chinese government. And we must be on guard against outright theft of our trade secrets and work to date. I've asked Emma Baumgartner to set up workshops in all our office locations. Her expert instructors will teach senior staff members about recognizing, reporting, and combatting industrial espionage.

"And, for a while anyway, we three guys and our executives, employees and consultants must be more vigilant about protecting our personal safety. I think we all need to get that message out, discreetly but clearly. Oh, and I've never had a proper succession plan, but I do now. I'll share that with you, Timofey, confidentially, since you have so graciously shared yours with me.

"Okay, let's address the meetings with G20 countries now…"

16

Excerpts from President Winslow's Afternoon Press Conference
Freeworld Press
White House
May 1, 2040

"Madam President, you said in your statement after the NATO Summit that the leaders of the free world would not be deterred by what you called cowardly acts of terrorism. Were you specifically referring to negative impact on the ZONT-2 project negotiations, or to something else?"

"It was a general, catch-all statement. But we continue to be intrigued by the L1 space umbrella and solar power plant idea."

"So, are we now actively negotiating with the ZONT-2 Corporation?"

"We are discussing ideas with them about how the US could participate, and benefit from involvement. Involvement could take many forms, and it must be in the best interest of the United States. I've asked Vice President Balaskas to spearhead those discussions."

"Madam President, there are rumours that the Chinese government could be behind two recent terrorist attacks. And that they keep trying to hack into government and corporate databases, especially targeting technical details about ZONT-2. Are these rumours true?"

"Our intelligence agencies are working closely with the intelligence agencies of our allies. When the full story is known, we will take the necessary actions to protect American interests, and as much as possible, the interests of our allies."

"But what if it *is* the Chinese government trying to outright kill the ZONT-2 project, or steal its hi-tech info, maybe so they can build their own space umbrella and solar power plant out there?"

"As you know, the State Department has been actively engaging with Chinese government officials at almost every level to see if we can end this wasteful and menacing cold war that seems to be raging between us. We remain hopeful that the UN and the other member countries of the G20 will help us with this effort."

"So, that's it? Just some diplomatic noises, and a few heated discussions with China's representative at G20 and UN meetings?"

"I can assure you, and the American people, that the US has the power and fortitude to respond to all forms of aggression, whether it be from a terrorist group or another nation. But where possible we prefer to use international law, the UN and other forums, economic levers, and peaceful, diplomatic means."

"So, you are confident Congress will support restoring or even bumping up our financial support for the UN?"

"Yes, it should be clear to everyone that the previous administration made a huge mistake withholding funds from the UN. I believe the UN could and should play a pivotal role in advancing potentially world-saving initiatives like this ZONT-2 project could turn out to be."

"Why aren't the other things we are doing to fight climate change working?"

"That is a great and highly complex question, and the last one I will take today. In a nutshell, the world has been consistently reluctant to do the necessary things. There are always excuses, like loss of existing jobs, or maybe it's not as bad as scientists say, or why should we do anything when some other countries do nothing, *et cetera, ad nauseum.*

"But the challenges *are* immense. Twenty years ago, only twenty percent of global energy demand was being met by electricity. In the US we have only managed to bump up electricity's share of our total energy supply and demand to thirty-five percent. A primary reason is the sheer scale of the problem.

"If we look back twenty years ago again, to completely replace the energy derived from burning carbon intensive fossil fuels, we would have had to expand the electrical grid five times! We are continuing to make our grid bigger, and smarter, but our own Congress is holding us back with endless political squabbles over funding. And the same political squabbles are occurring in most states.

"And that's just the grid I'm talking about! We must also proportionally expand our inventory of alternative energy sources. I'm talking about things like nuclear and renewables. So, if this ZONT-2 is indeed doable, and reliable, and economic, and most of all safe, it might indeed be a blessing. And that's what we must determine as soon as possible.

"Thank you, everyone, see you next time."

17

Alain Dufort and Gabriel Hofmann, the chief intelligence officer in the Swiss Federal Intelligence Service, were brusquely ushered into the Chinese Ambassador's office. The surprisingly austere office was in the Chinese Embassy in Bern, Switzerland. There was a Chinese national flag on a stand in a corner, and a very old portrait of Mao Zedong on a wall. Otherwise, the room looked like it was just a big empty closet.

The Chinese Ambassador to Switzerland, Guang Zhao, did not rise from his completely empty and puny desk to great his visitors. Instead, he simply watched as his attractive, petite, female assistant pulled two hard, well-worn, wooden chairs a few inches further away from the other side of his desk. And the three men all watched as the timid and nervous assistant hurriedly left the room and closed the door behind her. After an awkwardly long moment, Ambassador Zhao made a slow sweeping motion with his right hand, presumably indicating that Dufort and Hofmann should sit down opposite him.

When they were seated, Zhao said to them in English in a coarse, blunt manner, "What interest do you have with the People's Republic of China?"

Zhao's spoken English was known to always be pompous in tone, with a knife-like edge of hostility. He was sitting bolt upright with his back pressed firmly against his thinly cushioned leather chair. He was an overweight, balding, rather short fellow, with pale, waxy-looking skin.

"I am most interested in advancing discussions with the People's Republic of China about the nation's involvement in the ZONT-2 space umbrella and solar power project," Dufort answered formally in English without a hint of a smile. "And I have asked Gabriel here beside me to join us today, in case our discussion should partially involve intelligence matters."

"We have met before, Gabriel Hoffmann, here in this embassy, last year at our Chinese New Year's cocktail party. Your presence here today greatly puzzles me. Perhaps you can provide a better explanation than Monsieur Dufort just insultingly offered to me?"

"I am here to relay a message to China on behalf of the Swiss Federal Intelligence Agency, and allied intelligence agencies of some G20 member countries," Gabriel said clearly and forcefully. "We know China is sponsoring the terrorist organization UPKP. In fact, we know that China is using the UPKP as a mercenary force under the guise of fanatical religious terrorism to threaten nations interested in participating in the ZONT-2 project. China is also engaged in cyber-attacks against the ZONT-2 Corporation, and the Swiss, UK, EU, US and Russian governments. Every cyber-attack has originated in Shanghai or Hong Kong."

"You spout nothing but nonsense. The People's Republic of China fights its own battles. And we do not resort to cyber warfare. And it is no secret that we are considering leaving the G20. If your message is sincere, it could only accelerate our departure."

"Nevertheless, my message is that we are all watching China very closely, and we are prepared to counter further acts of aggression, violence and cyber-attacks, in kind."

"You are threatening China then, with violence and aggression, in some sort of spy war?"

"I have delivered the message as requested and urge you to relay it to higher Chinese authorities."

"Duly noted, as I note with disgust the arrogant and overly aggressive tone of your voice. And you, Monsieur Dufort, you also have a message for me, or for China, perhaps?"

"Yes, I do. My first message is that I do not wish to talk to a closed door any more. I believe it is in China's best interest to seriously consider entering partnering discussions with ZONT-2 Corporation. Good business is good business, and there is no reason for such hostility towards us. We believe we are on track to have participation agreements with the other G20 countries fully in place by the end of the year.

"Every nation in the world including China needs to stop burning coal and other forms of hydrocarbons. The pollution in China is killing people. Climate change is also killing Chinese people, and starvation in your nation caused by widespread crop failures has never been worse.

Virtually unlimited clean energy is the solution to many problems. So is a space-based, solar umbrella to combat or even reverse climate change. But no corporation or nation on Earth could build ZONT-2 on its own, including China. And the nations of the world would never tolerate a ZONT-2 facility that was controlled exclusively by one country.

"My second and last message is related to the first. Wardenclyffe Corporation would welcome the possibility of re-entering the business world in China, through joint ventures again if that is the only possible way. The supply chain supporting ZONT-2 will be enormous, and China would benefit tremendously through friendly and ethical participation in that supply chain. But it must play fair, and not engage in the theft of knowledge, arrest of employees for political leverage, or other bully tactics."

"I cannot foresee how Wardenclyffe would ever be welcome back in China. Wardenclyffe is a blatantly capitalistic and imperialistic exploiter of working-class people, and its continued existence is the reason the Chinese Revolution must continue and at an accelerated pace. China has been around for thousands of years. It has always looked to itself for solutions, and it will keep doing so because it works so well. It is the world that must change, not China. Communism is the answer, not capitalism. Capitalism is destroying the world, and China is just trying to survive in a world of hostile, capitalistic and imperialistic enemies."

"So, you are saying the world is the bully, not China?"

"In essence, yes. Furthermore, China will never buy electrical power from a non-state-owned corporation, especially a foreign, obviously capitalistic corporation."

"I see. Then that will do it for today, Mister Ambassador. Will you relay Gabriel Hoffman's message to higher Chinese authorities? And my two messages as well?"

Guang Zhao simply glared back at the two men sitting on the other side of his desk.

Alain decided to play one more card. He forced a smile, and said, "What if we assure you, Mister Ambassador, that we will never tell anyone about this conversation? And, if we further assure you that no government or spy agency will ever talk about it either?"

"Then I may *possibly* relay your messages," Guang Zhao replied with a bit of a sarcastic snort. "And I agree this discussion never happened. Is that all for today? This has been a most annoying non-discussion."

"Are we finished here, Gabriel? A quick nod means yes in my book. Okay, so now we will leave your esteemed presence, Ambassador Zhao. Do not trouble yourself, I think we will eventually find our own way out of your embassy. But it might be better if your pretty assistant led the way for us and cleared us through security again. Would that be possible?"

"That is her job. I have already given the order."

18

Larry Rhodes was getting set to open a political rally in Austin, Texas. He watched as the crowd continued to pour into the stadium stands around the college football field. He was pleased to see most folks were wearing his red cowboy hats, as he had encouraged them to do on his most recent, radio talk show. Larry's show was syndicated, and popular in traditionally red party, right-leaning states.

It was a poorly kept secret that Larry intended to run for President of the United States. But right now, he was intent on stroking the most extreme right-wing elements of American society under the guise of supporting red party congressional candidates in the upcoming mid-term elections. He also figured the gullible folks that came to these rallies and listened without fail to his radio shows would support him as well when he officially announced he was in the running for the nation's highest office.

Larry did not believe most of the stuff he said on his talk shows, or at these political rallies. In fact, most of it was made up. He had always been a compulsive and possibly pathological liar. But today his mission was purposeful. He intended to throw out trial balloons to test what views were popular with the political base. And he was well rewarded for his probing by the red, right-wing party. His fees were atrociously high, and they paid him on time without complaint.

Larry desperately needed the money he received from these unruly propaganda gigs. He was addicted to gambling, and the casinos, not surprisingly, always won when looked at in aggregate. And he had tried to get rich by starting up small companies that peddled everything from sandals to non-prescription sleeping pills to sleeping bags. And all those businesses had failed.

Larry's latest business venture was peddling the red cowboy hats with the big and bold 'I'M A MERKAN' gold-lettered logo. He needed this scam to work, and things were looking hopeful, judging by tonight's crowd. Supposedly the proceeds would all flow into red party coffers, but actually the cash was all going to end up in Larry's pocket. The money should then have been passed on to his two ex-wives for the support of four hungry kids. But Larry had already forgotten he was a deadbeat father.

However, Larry's first wife had not forgotten the sick way Larry had ogled and even fondled their very pretty and oldest, barely teenaged daughter, and this ex-wife had successfully obtained a restraining order to keep Larry away.

As Larry strutted up the stairs to the stage and over to the podium wearing his never-been-soiled cowboy chaps, the crowd erupted with 'Moo! Moo!' cattle calls, hoots and hollers, and cowboy cheers like 'Yahoo!'. He smiled broadly, and waved for a few minutes, pointing at people in the crowd that he pretended to recognize. Then as the cheering started to die down, he adjusted the microphone on the podium and began his introductory speech:

"Howdy, folks! It sure looks like the eyes of Texas are upon me! And shucks, y'all, I love it! And I love all of you, too!

"So, here we all are in the grand old city of Austin, Texas! Boy, there's a lot of history here, and a fine university, and a lot of hi-tech businesses. You would think Stephen F. Austin and Sam Houston would be proud. But they ain't, because the blue treasonous fools in Washington are letting the Chinese design their space-based phaser starship just up the road from here. And their phasers won't be on stun, believe you me!

"Officially, it's going to be a space umbrella and a solar powerplant, the brainchild of a Russian and a French guy, or maybe he's Swiss, or whatever. But don't y'all believe that! They're all lying, like they lie about everything else. The Chinese are behind it all, believe me, just like they were behind the last two pandemics. They want to blackmail places like Texas with their illegal space weapon. But we're not fooled, are we! Texans aren't fools! And another thing, they think the South China Sea is theirs just because the name has China in it! They built three more islands out there to stake their phony claim. I tell you what, I'd nuke them all if I could.

"But we're here to listen to what a fine upstanding candidate for the US Senate thinks about all of this, not me. I'm just the warm-up act.

"Yes? Oh, okay, they're telling me in my earphone that I've got a few more minutes.

"So, they make cars here, too, did you know that? Korean ones, or maybe they're Chinese, probably Chinese, but what's the difference? They all look the same, right? And you know I'm not just talking about the cars, chuckle, chuckle. Electric cars, I hear, but that's okay, maybe. I've never believed in all that climate change garbage, no, sir, never did. But electric cars? Well, whatever, I guess.

"By the way, we'll just have to see if the climate actually does change. And what's wrong with warmer anyway? Texans like hot weather and hot food. And cold beer to wash it down. But we'll see. We'll see what happens.

"But here we are, and it's great! And you're great, and I'm great. And America's great. And some day you may even want me to be your President. But we'll see, we'll see what happens.

"So, that's what forty-thousand patriotic people look like! They told me that was the head count for tonight. Seems much bigger than that. But shucks, still, what a great turn out! And we've got live music coming up soon. Both kinds. Country and western! So, thanks for coming, folks!

"Oh, it looks like our famous Mister Blaze needs a few more minutes to get ready. So, what else should we talk about? Elections maybe. Everyone knows when the red party loses, the election was rigged by the blue party. All we can hope for is that we can scare them away sometimes and take a few House and Senate seats. And that President in the White House, she sure never got there legitimately. There will be a day of reckoning, believe you me, like when the valiant red protesters almost took over Congress way back in 2020.

"Should we talk about Mexicans too, for a spell? Now, as for the Mexicans, they still need to be put in their place. And I mean for ever and ever. We kept building bigger walls, but we just could not keep them out. They're like rats sneaking into our country. At night because they're all cowards. And they're all drug dealers and pimps. And they molest children. Bad people. Very bad. Believe me.

"So, the Mexicans and the Chinese and the warmongers that want to build that monstrosity of a starship better watch out! Who do they think they're messing with? Don't ever mess with Texas!

"Okay, it looks like that's it for me, and darn it, I was just getting on a roll, too. So, let's hear a good old Texas cheer for our next Senator, the brilliant, the range-smart, the rooting and the tooting, and the former world champion bull rider... Mister Beau Blaze!"

19

The harbour in Beirut, Lebanon had never been fully rebuilt after the horrific explosion that occurred there on August 4, 2020. The explosion had been fuelled by two thousand seven hundred and fifty tonnes of improperly stored ammonium nitrate. It was one of the most powerful artificial non-nuclear explosions in history. No one had ever been convicted of negligence or an act of terrorism. And Lebanon itself was still a dangerous, corrupt, impoverished, possibly ungovernable place, although a democracy of sorts still existed.

Yitzchak Ben Dod was sitting beside his young Christian Arab driver in a large, one-tonne capacity, un-roofed jeep parked in a concealed spot overlooking Beirut harbour and a dilapidated dock. Behind them in the jeep stood another young Arab man, a Shia Muslim, whose job was to operate a twin-barrelled, fifty-calibre machine gun that was mounted on a sturdy, swivelling pedestal.

It was coming up on two o'clock in the morning and it was pitch black everywhere. The jeep was positioned between two rusty shipping containers. In the gap between two other containers about one hundred metres to their right was another jeep fitted out with a bank of halogen floodlights. There was no one in that jeep.

Yitzchak was an agent of Mossad, the Israeli intelligence agency. His assistants were reliable, patriotic mercenaries, who hated terrorist groups of all types. Like most young Lebanese, they were completely fed up with the lawlessness of Beirut. The obvious analogy with Tombstone, Arizona in the days of the wild west led Yitzchak to name his driver Doc Holliday, and his machine-gunner Wyatt Earp. The two men liked the code names. There was a third man, a Sunni Arab, hidden down on the dock. He was an expert in three martial arts, and he preferred to kill with his hands. For this assignment, they called him Virgil Earp. And his job was to apprehend, not kill, the suspect when he appeared as anticipated on the dock. And the suspect was known to Mossad as a UPKP terrorist.

As it slipped past two a.m., the three men in the jeep started to get apprehensive. At quarter past two, the three men were wondering if something had gone wrong. But then Yitzchak heard in his tiny headset speakers in stilted English, "I've got Billy Clanton, boss. I may have broken his right arm... but I cuffed him anyway. And he's gagged... of course. He never made a sound. But he's squealing a bit now. There... that head smack probably knocked him out for a while."

"Thanks, that's great, Virgil," Yitzhak replied quietly, also in English. "We certainly didn't hear anything up here. Stay under cover. A *lot* of cover. There could be a lot of shooting soon, and a bloody big bang or two."

"Right, boss."

Yitzchak waited a few minutes for Virgil to get himself and his captive into a safer place. Then he turned to his driver and said in English, "Hit the switch, Doc."

The bank of floodlights on the other jeep lit up instantly and caught the outline of a rusty, black, completely unlit, fishing trawler. It was about twenty metres out from the dock, and quietly using its side thrusters to come right along side the broken-down wharf.

"Open up, Wyatt!" Yitzhak yelled.

A few moments after Wyatt had started pummeling the trawler with massive, high-velocity bullets, a twenty-millimetre calibre cannon mounted aft of the trawler's bridge started popping off rounds at the bank of flood lights. Wyatt corrected his aim and took out the cannon operator just as the flood lights went dark. But it did not matter now. There were tracer rounds mixed in with the .50 BMG rounds. And the trawler was now lit up with fires and glowing smoke from stem to stern.

"That's enough for the bridge, start aiming for the containers on the deck, Wyatt!"

"Right, boss!" Wyatt yelled back.

Suddenly the trawler blew up. The shock wave knocked Wyatt off the back of the jeep, and some shrapnel shattered but did not break the jeep's windshield.

After another minute, Wyatt had climbed back on to the back of the jeep. He bravely nodded to Yitzhak to indicate he was okay, but he looked a bit stunned. Then Yitzhak said quietly, "Okay, turn on the jeep's headlights, Doc."

When the halon, full-intensity beams on the jeep were burning bright, they could see that there was really nothing but smoke, flotsam and jetsam where the trawler had been, and there was a lot of fresh debris on the dock.

"Virgil, are you okay?" Yitzhak asked quietly into his headset microphone. He didn't even try to hide his anguish. After a few moments he said more loudly, "Come on, Virgil, tell me you're all right, buddy."

"Yeah, we're... we're both all right, but that was a hell of a wallop, boss."

"Okay, get yourself and your captive up to the jeep as fast as you can. I hear sirens, and we've got to boogey our butts out of here, and pronto, Kemosabe."

20

It was almost eleven-thirty am Moscow time on June 3, 2040. Acting on independent tips from both the GRU, or the Main Intelligence Directorate, and the FSB, or the Federal Security Bureau, uniformed and heavily armed officers of the Moscow City Police Force, and the Russian Federal Police Force, quickly and efficiently set up two more barricades. They blocked the eastern entranceways to both the Slavyanskaya Hotel and the PlasTekhKorp Tower, located to the west of central Moscow. Two other barricades had already been set up to block the approaches to the area from the west.

The cordoned off area was just south of the busy Kievsky Railway Station, so the traffic was heavy. On a signal from a Russian Police Force coordinator, the officers simultaneously began stopping cars and trucks at all the barricades. They checked identification cards and turned away every non-suspicious vehicle. A few vehicles were directed to improvised marshalling areas, where drivers, passengers and vehicles were thoroughly searched.

At five minutes before noon at one of the eastern barricades, a natural-gas powered two-and-a-half tonne panel truck was motioned forward by a Moscow traffic-department police officer. But instead of moving forward, the truck went hard into reverse, crushing the front end of the Volga electric taxicab behind it. Then the truck lurched forward to the left so it could start a three-point turnaround. It ran over a Russian Criminal Department Police Officer who had his hands held high up in the air while yelling for the driver to stop the truck. All the police officers at the barricade then began firing at the cab of the vehicle with pistols and automatic assault rifles, but the bullets harmlessly bounced off what looked to be armoured glass and metal. The truck managed to complete its violent, evasive manoeuvre, but in the process, it crushed a small private electric car, killing its female driver and her child passenger.

The truck accelerated northwards but suddenly the roadway was blocked by police cars hurriedly parked sideways in the road. The truck rammed the improvised barrier of police cars at high speed, but it rode up on one of the cars and became stuck with its front bumper high up in the air. The driver of the truck frantically tried to reverse off the crushed car that had become wedged underneath it. The rear tyres smoked, bounced and screeched like a dragster at the start of a drag race, but the heavy vehicle was obviously pinned in place. Police officers quickly surrounded the truck with their pistols and assault rifles aimed at the cab. They barked orders for the male driver and his male passenger to get out of the truck with their hands up.

Suddenly the truck exploded. The horrific blast completely levelled the area, killing and wounding hundreds of police officers and civilians. Some of the injuries and two of the fatalities were from flying glass when some windows in the nearby Kievsky Railway Station were blown inwards.

After a four-hour delay, the UPKP terrorist group claimed responsibility for the massacre on social media. They spoke again of a holy jihad against ZONT-2, which they said they were leading on behalf of all Islamic people.

The Russian media was quick to label the attack as the senseless work of madmen, or deranged domestic terrorists, without offering any proof. They pointed out that UPKP's claim made little sense. They asked how killing hundreds of Russian police officers and civilians could possibly help them with their cause or be in any way something that Islamic people would support. Social media blogs agreed there was nothing holy about what happened. And bloggers argued ZONT-2 was a way to save the world from human-caused climate change, and they asked why any rational person would want to stop it. Moscow's Mayor announced that the cause espoused by UPKP was the work of the devil.

The Russian government said it was a cowardly, violent act that probably missed its intended target, but it did not say what that target might have been.

The Moscow city first responders took injured people to suddenly over-crowded hospitals, and dead people to over-crowded morgues. The forensic experts on the Russian police force quickly announced there really wasn't much left to analyze. The blast was thought to have been about the size of the Oklahoma City, USA bombing of April 19, 1995. Lab testing of samples near ground zero, and analysis of the geometry and extent of the blast damage, suggested perhaps a tonne of ammonium nitrate fertilizer had been mixed with half a tonne of hydrazine rocket fuel to make the bomb. That information was not shared with the media or the public. Physical damage was estimated to be in the order of a billion US dollars. City workers and utility workers spent the next three weeks clearing debris and restoring services to the area. The Kievsky Railway Station was operating two days after the blast using alternate entrance and exit roadways.

21

CIA Director Margaret Dabrowski half-jogged and half-sprinted down the wide White House hallway to catch up with the President's National Security Advisor, Bertrand Latimore. Bertrand was walking at a very brisk pace. They were both empty-handed. When Margaret was beside him, Bertrand said between quick breaths, "Thanks for joining me... with no notice, Margaret. The President and her Chief of Staff are both tied up today... with the Saudi and Indian state visits... all related to ZONT-2 and trade with China. She asked that we brief the Vice President... about what we think is going on with this UPKP bunch. Then he'll update her... at their next scheduled overlap. Okay?"

"Yes, I'm ready," she replied with a bit of a gasp herself. "I knew someone would be asking us for a briefing."

Christos Balaskas got back to his office just moments before Bertrand and Margaret arrived. He was going to sit down at his desk, but then he impulsively changed his mind and said with a quick laugh, "No, on second thought, let's all sit down at the round table, King Arthur style, shall we?"

Bertrand had heard his little joke before, but he responded with a dutiful chuckle. Margaret's demeanor remained stoic as always.

"You two look a bit winded," Christos began when they were all seated. He had a little note pad in front of him, and a pencil in his right hand. "Sorry to put you out like this. But you know it's important. And this gap just appeared in my schedule out of nowhere."

"No problem, Chris," Bertrand responded amiably. "Yes, there's a lot going on, and all of it important. Margaret, would you kick this off for us, please?"

"Sure thing, Bert. I've just about got my breath back after my clumsy sprint. Chris, you are probably aware that the UPKP terrorist group claimed on social media that they were responsible for the devastating Moscow massacre. They spoke again of a holy jihad against ZONT-2, which they say they are leading. They did not say what their target specifically was in Moscow, but there can be little doubt it was the PlasTekhKorp Tower."

"Before you go on, Margaret, I don't believe anyone has ever explained to me what the letters UPKP stand for. It must be an acronym of sorts, only a translation from Arabic, perhaps?"

"No, Chris. Apparently, it is a sick, perverted English word acronym. They are the United People Killing People. As such, there is a message there for all to see. The affiliation with a religion like Islam, or a branch of Islam, is just a façade. They are hired guns, or bombers, and that's it.

"Now, UPKP does not seem intent on targeted assassinations to derail or decapitate the promoters of the ZONT-2 project. Alain Dufort and Timofey Semenov would probably be dead by now if that were the case, despite the elaborate security measures they make for themselves, and what their host governments provide to them. Rather, UPKP seems to think broader, psychological warfare will get more and more people, a.k.a. voters in democratic countries, thinking it is just not worth it to continue. In other words, they use mayhem to create political problems for leaders in industrialized nations, and more specifically, for the leaders of the influential member countries of the G20, and the UN Security Council.

"Russia's FSB, or Federal Security Bureau, believes the two men in the truck that blew up were suicide bombers. They were said to be Chechens who were frustrated that the armed Islamic State group has been effectively neutered in Dagestan. The Russian government has not revealed their belief to the Russian public, however, as they fear it could encourage all the ethnically Chechen, Sharia Law advocating terror groups, to start up again.

"The two young men were not just known to the FSB and the Russian Federal Police. They were actively recruited by the UPKP and convinced somehow that their ultimate sacrifice would save the world, and by extension, Chechens.

"The discovery that the massive bomb was made from ammonium nitrate fertilizer and hydrazine is highly relevant. Rocket launching companies now only use non-polluting liquid hydrogen and liquid oxygen. The exhaust from such rocket engines is just non-polluting water in the form of hypersonic steam, and heat. Solid-propellent, expendable side-boosters are also used, but they don't use hydrazine. Only China is using the hypergolic fuel hydrazine in some of its rockets. And hydrazine is very expensive. It has specialized industrial applications as well, and China is now the number one producer and consumer of the toxic stuff.

"So, China is again suspected of backing and financing what UPKP is doing. And there was another explosion that you may not have heard about that effectively confirms this suspicion.

"The Canadian Security Intelligence Service, or CSIS, alerted us, and other allied intelligence services, including Israel's Mossad, of a suspicious cargo that was loaded on to a smallish cargo ship in the port of Vancouver, British Colombia. The cargo only consisted of Canadian-manufactured ammonium nitrate fertilizer and Chinese-manufactured hydrazine. The paper trail, the money trail and coordinated tracking by allied navies and coast guards, confirm that the ship then made its way through the Panama Canal, across the Atlantic Ocean, and then into the Mediterranean Sea. Italian Coast Guard patrol planes with infrared cameras watched it offload drums and containers to a Lebanese-registered fishing trawler in the dark of night, at sea, twenty-three nautical miles south of Sicily. The allied intelligence agencies then agreed with us that we should all carefully watch the trawler's next move, as it could reveal something more interesting. When it was certain the trawler was headed to Beirut, Lebanon, Mossad went into high gear.

"The Mossad captured a UPKP terrorist on the Beirut dock where the trawler was about to offload its cargo. It all happened at about two in the morning on June 1, or five days ago. In the process of making their capture, machine gun and or cannon fire was exchanged with the trawler, and it blew up, or rather part of the cargo it was carrying blew up. The rest went into the sea and is being recovered by the unsuspecting Lebanese authorities. They are telling the press they are at a loss to explain the explosion, as they have been saying for years about the much bigger blast that occurred way back in 2020.

"Mossad covertly took the captured terrorist back to Israel. It borders with Lebanon, and the border is porous for experienced intelligence agencies like Mossad. The captive man confessed that the UPKP was going to use a huge truck bomb to attack the Tel Aviv government complex. When he was asked why he and the UPKP would want to do such a thing, he said it was all part of saving the world. And, as a sidebar, he said that really hurting the infidel Jewish state was, quote, 'always a good sport'. The suspect also apparently revealed details about how UPKP is organized. Mossad refuses to tell anybody else about that part, and now intends to take matters into its own hands. It also refused to reveal if the suspect survived the interrogation methods that were employed to extract his confession."

"Okay, I think that summarizes the latest from my end."

"Thanks, Margaret, and I can add a bit to that, Chris," Bertrand quickly interjected before Christos could respond. "We simply cannot let Mossad handle this point forward. We need a higher level discussion to occur between Israel and the United States. I'm thinking perhaps at our Secretary of State level, and the Israeli equivalent. We believe UPKP is a large organization, with small cells that are geographically dispersed across northern Africa and the Middle East but controlled from bases in Libya. Mossad probably intends to assassinate their leader, which frankly will not be enough. We'll need to eradicate their logistical and military apparatus as well. And we are well positioned and fully capable of doing that. Our armed forces are still the best in the world, with the best hi-tech gadgetry."

"I agree, Bert," Christos replied immediately. "And if China is sponsoring and supplying this UPKP group, and they see it being systematically dismantled, we will want them to know for certain that the full might of the US is firmly behind it all. The President thinks our relationship must get worse with China before it can get better. But this could, and probably will, push us to the brink of a major conflagration, and it must be handled very carefully."

"Sorry, you two, but that's all the time I can spare for you right now. I'm back-filling for President Kate again while she's heads down with other pressing matters. But what you have told me has moved to the top of the list of stuff I will address with her and the White House Chief of Staff when next we meet. So, thanks again, and off you go to your appointed tasks, and me to chair a close, probably deadlocked, Senate vote."

22

Chinese Ambassador Jia Yongkang's Speech
UN General Assembly
June 22, 2040
Freeworld Press English Translation

"I will begin with a statement of facts, and then address the reckless rhetoric and string of lies that the US Ambassador just inflicted on this once venerable General Assembly.

"China is not the enemy of the so-called free world. But China can and will defend itself from aggression in any form. And those capitalists and exploiters promoting this ZONT-2 energy beam weapon in the guise of a power plant, or some sort of world-saving sunscreen, are clearly liars and aggressors.

"The Chinese Communist Party made a grave mistake when it experimented with so called limited capitalism. The argument that capitalism is the first stage of communism was flawed. At first glance, the goal seemed admirable, that is, to develop Chinese industrial capacity for technical and commercial advantage. We dominated world trade for decades. We showed the weaknesses inherent with capitalism, and the flaccid aggressors we intimidated responded with ill-conceived and inflammatory tariffs and sanctions against China. In other words, we failed to expand the Chinese Revolution beyond our borders.

"The Chinese Communist Party once again at long last believes wholeheartedly that Marxism-Leninism reveals the universal laws governing the development of a truly human society. 'Mao Zedong Thought' is an integration of the universal truth of Marxism-Leninism with the practice of the Chinese Revolution. 'Mao Zedong Thought' also seeks truth from facts. And the hardest fact that has been re-learned is that China is isolated in the world. It can trust no other country. And it will now further expand its already massive military might to combat untruth and aggression in all their many guises. And the imperialist running dogs within the Chinese Communist Party and within aggressor nations will be running scared again. And they had best run fast to escape our wrath.

"China has been accused once again, just now, by the US Ambassador of being a terror state, and that we hire terrorists to do our so-called dirty work. The members of the UN Security Council are behaving like imperialist running dogs by agreeing with this lie. The Chinese Communist Party no longer sees value in remaining a member of this so-called security council or remaining a member of the capitalistic G20 pack of feral mongrel dogs. All these groups do is provide a vehicle for our aggressors to foam at their rabid dog lips as they spout their endless string of lies against us.

"China will remain a member of this General Assembly, for a while longer perhaps. We may have a few friends left in the world. To test that possibility, I invite the Ambassadors for North Korea, Vietnam and Cuba to now reaffirm to this General Assembly their allegiance to the universal truth of Marxism-Leninism and join China in renouncing this ZONT-2 space weapon."

23

Alain Dufort was sitting by himself at a corner table in a quiet, posh, martini bar in Hotel des Bergues in Geneva, Switzerland. It was late in the afternoon, and Alain had just finished a long, gruelling workday filled with difficult meetings. The last meeting had occurred in the hotel he was now sitting in, where he kept a business centre and an apartment-like suite.

Alain was dressed like he was about to play golf at a high-end club, even though he hated the game, and he had no time for it anyway. His plain-clothed, personal security guard, Benoit Duplantier, was sitting on a cushioned bar stool with his back to the wall at the extreme left end of the bar. Benoit was watching everything that was happening around him very closely, without looking like he was doing so.

Alain noted there was a beautiful young lady sitting by herself at the extreme right end of the bar. She had long black hair, and she was wearing a sexy, form-fitting, lacy black dress with a revealing decolletage. Alain could not help but notice that she had a lot to reveal. Suddenly their eyes met, and Alain realized that he had seen the woman two days before, in a first-class lounge bar in Geneva Airport. Their eyes had briefly met then and there, too.

The young lady broke off her stare without showing any emotional response and went back to typing something into her smart phone. Then Alain picked up his smart phone and dialled up Benoit. When Benoit answered with his ultra-secure cell phone, they had a quiet and quick, back-and-forth exchange. Then Benoit hung up, stood up, put his phone in the back pocket of his designer jeans, and casually strolled down to the other end of the bar.

"I am sorry to bother you, mademoiselle or madame," he said quietly to the young lady in French. "My name is Benoit Duplantier. I work for Alain Dufort. He is the gentleman sitting by himself in the corner of the bar room. He is very famous, and he thinks you may have recognized him. He was hoping you might like to have a drink with him, and a little chat."

She looked a bit startled when Benoit had first approached her. But now she smiled politely, and replied quietly in French, "Yes, I might like that, Benoit."

"That's marvellous. And how should I introduce you to Monsieur Dufort?"

"As Mei Wu-Toussaint, without a preceding mademoiselle or madame."

"That's perfectly acceptable, of course. Please, let's go meet Alain. You might not know, I suppose, that he is the wealthiest and most powerful person on the planet."

Mei did not react to Benoit's remarkable description of Alain. She simply said, "Yes, please, let's do that, Benoit."

Benoit followed Mei over to Alain's table. Alain rose to his feet, and Benoit said over Mei's right shoulder in French, "Monsieur Dufort, may I introduce to you a charming young lady? Her name is Mei Wu-Toussaint."

"Yes, you certainly may, Benoit," Alain replied in his native Swiss version of French. "I hope you will not be offended by my brashness, but would you join me, Mei, for a drink and a little chat?"

"Yes, I would be pleased to do so, Monsieur Dufort," Mei replied in French with a Parisian accent.

Benoit strode forward and pulled out the chair at the table that was directly opposite Alain. He smoothly pushed the chair in for Mei as she was sitting down, and then he returned to his watch station at the left end of the bar.

Alain smiled, and said, "Please, call me Alain. And what will you have, Mei? It will be my treat."

"What have you just finished drinking, Alain?"

"A dry gin martini, on the rocks, with a twist of lime."

"Then I'll have one of those as well. Thank you."

Alain flashed a vee-sign to Benoit at the bar and held up his empty glass. The hand signal had two traditional meanings of course, but Benoit simply nodded and placed the drink order with the bartender.

Alain smiled again at Mei, a little coyly this time, and said, "You might not believe this Mei, but it is not my way to pick up women in bars."

"Yes, I know. I have studied your ways. And before you ask, yes, we have met before, or at least our eyes have met before."

"In the first-class lounge at Geneva airport. I was departing for Paris."

"Yes, on your Arrow II business jet. I was off to Paris as well, on Air France."

"You *do* know a lot about me, it seems. And how is that?"

Before Mei could answer, the bartender arrived with their drinks, and said in French, "A Tanqueray dry gin martini on the rocks with a twist of lime for you, madame. And one for you as well, monsieur. And I'll take away that empty glass for you, monsieur. Enjoy."

When the bartender was back behind the bar, Mei replied, "I wrote a paper on you when I did my MBA at the University of Paris. You never fly commercial."

"That's right, Mei. And may I observe that your name is an interesting amalgam of French and Chinese? Does it reflect your heritage?"

"Yes, Alain. My father was the Chinese Ambassador to France. My mother was his mistress. When I was ten years old, he told his superiors that he wanted to marry my mother and spend more time with his wife and daughter. They immediately recalled him to Beijing. And we never saw or heard from him again."

Alain paused to digest that disturbing bit of information, and to more closely study Mei's pretty face. She remained stoic, and impossible to read. So, he replied, "That's a terribly sad story, Mei. But you seem to have made a life for yourself."

"Yes, thanks, I have. My father was basically married to my mother, and I loved him dearly. They had a joint bank account. And when he left for Beijing, my mother *de facto* inherited the full fortune, which was considerable. There was more than enough to start me on my way. My mother died last year, so I have what remains of the family fortune now."

"So, a clear connection with China. You are the daughter of a Chinese Ambassador who was undoubtedly an inner party member. And you are independently wealthy. That is all most interesting, Mei. And I'm starting to suspect that our meeting is not by chance. Am I correct?"

"Yes, you are, Alain."

"So, you don't always dress so enticingly, and visit martini bars by yourself either, I suppose."

"No. I have a live-in man friend, and this was all done to catch your eye and set-up a private, seemingly innocuous conversation."

"Well, I guess I can get over that profound disappointment, but only if our innocuous conversation turns out to be worthwhile. So, are you working for your own interests, or someone else's?"

"Both. You see, I am mostly here to deliver a message from high-ranking members of the Chinese Communist Party who are *disgruntled*, shall we say, using a phonetically interesting English word, with the current leadership in China. These people would be some of the, quote, 'imperialist running dogs' that Ambassador Jia Yongkang referred to in his speech at the UN last week. His insulting and comically childish terminologies are archaic, but they aptly reflect the political regression that has been going on in China."

"The US government is also seriously *disgruntled*, shall we also say again in English, with Chinese leadership, Mei. My intelligence community contact told me that Yongkang's tyrannical speech sent the US military to DEFCON4, or above normal readiness. Practically, it means increased intelligence surveillance and strengthened security measures. But it is also a warning to China that a cold war can quickly escalate and get out of hand, and that words matter.

"Speaking of words, and as a side thought, Mei, I have always wondered if *gruntlement* is the opposite of *disgruntlement*. And if you know me as well as you say, you could never imagine me caring too much about someone else's *gruntlement*, especially if that person was my estranged wife.

"But back to our conversation, and leaving behind my crude attempt at wit, how did you get wrapped-up with these people? Are you a communist?"

"No, I'm not a communist *per se*. But I lean appreciably far to the left, like a lot of French people do. I have a bachelor's degree in environmental engineering as well, and I have always been active in the green movement."

"So, in a nutshell, can I presume that you would like to see our ZONT-2 project move forward?"

"I desperately want to see it move forward, Alain."

"Okay, that's good. And what is the message you are here to deliver to me?"

"The secret counterrevolutionaries want you to know there will undoubtedly be a coup in China, probably within the next six months. They know that most intellectuals in China favour participation in the ZONT-2 project, but are afraid to speak out, fearing the inevitable and sometimes fatal repercussions. But no one would want ZONT-2 to be operated by a capitalist, profit-seeking corporation, like yours, or like the joint venture corporation that you and Timofey Semenov created, and that Holt Carson runs for you."

"Oh, I see. And what would be an acceptable alternative for yourself, and these dissenting people, who are presumably members of the Politburo in China?"

"We are wondering if you would consider restructuring the board of directors of your joint venture corporation to allow the world to effectively own and run the company."

"What exactly are you talking about?"

"We are talking about putting in place twelve directors, appointed by twelve influential countries that would in turn be accountable to the majority viewpoint of nations in defined regions of the world."

"And which countries are we talking about?"

"Canada, the USA, Brazil, Argentina, the UK, the EU countries in aggregate, South Africa, Saudi Arabia, Russia, China, India and Australia."

"An interesting mix. Sort of has a UN feel to it, only a lot smaller. Why would it be unacceptable to just make, say, the UN Security Council the joint venture corporation's board of directors?"

"There are fifteen members on the UN Security Council, and only five are permanent members who were picked after the Second World War for outdated political reasons. You know full well that an effective board of directors needs to be smaller, and stable, composed of competent, objective and experienced people capable of overseeing the activities of a large corporation. And China is not alone in thinking that the UN Security Council has been a disaster. It needs to be reformed for the UN to survive."

"Okay. Noted. Perhaps you and the conspirators in China know that our strategy has been to try to sign up G20 countries, believing they have the financial resources and the influencing power to enable the project to at least get started. Are you saying, metaphorically, that we have been barking up the wrong tree, as running or rabid feral dogs might do, perhaps?"

"No, we're saying you will never get started on your mega project without an authorizing UN resolution by the General Assembly. This is about updating space laws which have not kept up with technology. That means fifty percent of the General Assembly must vote in favour of the resolution or overriding space law, plus at least one vote. You should be trying to tentatively sign up as many countries as you can to commercial agreements and starting with the G20 countries sounds reasonable. But you won't get China, or the US onboard for that matter, if you are proposing to run ZONT-2 as a private and profit-focussed venture. And I imagine the EU will balk at that proposal, too."

"So, how would Wardenclyffe and PlasTekhKorp fit into all of this?"

"They would be the prime service providers to the joint venture corporation for a defined, first stage of the project. Competitive bidding would occur before the next stage was approved. You would be well positioned to compete in the next bidding round. And you would make a lot of money in any stage of the project, especially if it required say three to five years to complete."

"There may be something to what you say, Mei. I will share with you that some of the EU nations have only been making a few timid supportive noises in our discussions with them so far. We have indeed heard some negative noises from the US. And the US has had its own issues over the last few decades. The place is politically polarized, with just red and blue and no purple. The opposition to ZONT-2 is fuelled by fake news, and paranoia about foreign domination, especially by China.

Racism is undoubtedly an underlying root cause, unfortunately, and that human failing is not something one can simply negotiate away.

"But I will carefully consider what you have just said to me. And I sincerely thank you for doing so, Mei."

"You are most welcome, Alain. Do you think you might discuss this matter and opportunity with Timofey Semenov and Holt Carson?"

"I probably will. Yes, I think so. And will we be able to discuss it again?"

"I think so. Yes. As long as our relationship remains platonic."

"Yes, well, I enjoy a similar relationship with another beautiful lady. It seems to be my fate or curse in life. So, why don't we exchange email addresses? We would only exchange a few pleasantries and allude to a possible get-together, and then subsequently agree when and where to meet exactly through intermediaries. Neither of us should ever trust cybersecurity implicitly."

"Okay, that sounds fine."

"And would you like another martini? My limit is two, but my arm may be bendable just now."

"And my limit is one, but if we both drink them very slowly, I am agreeable."

"Okay." Another vee-sign to Benoit, and a raised empty glass. "There, done. He's a sharp lad, that one. Now tell me about this man-friend of yours, and how he got to be so lucky…"

24

The Joint Chiefs of Staff of the United States of America scrambled to assemble for an emergency meeting in the Pentagon. It was 14:05 EDT on July 23, 2040. Admiral Hiram Nichols chaired the impromptu session as the highest-ranking officer in the US armed forces. When all the generals and admirals were seated around a long table in their situation room, Admiral Nichols barked, "I have asked Rear Admiral Bud Gammon along with my people to brief us on the escalating situation in the South China Sea. Go ahead, Bud."

"Thank you, Admiral. I'll start right in. We all know the South China Sea is a vital waterway. A third of the world's shipping passes through it every year. China has been building artificial islands there and violating international law by declaring twelve-mile territorial limits around those islands. This week we have been conducting man overboard drills near their newest island in the Spratly Island chain. This is a standard exercise to demonstrate the Navy's ability to operate effectively in international waters.

"We deployed ships from the US Seventh Fleet for the exercises, specifically the *USS Barack Obama* fleet aircraft carrier, two guided missile cruisers, four guided missile frigates, two attack submarines, five mine sweepers and two supply and fuel tenders. The exercises were being performed in conjunction with ships of the Australian and Indonesian navies.

"The *HMAS Dingo*, an Australian Anzac II class frigate, was being shadowed by a Chinese frigate for over fifty nautical miles on its port side. Yesterday morning at zero-six-hundred hours local time, the Chinese frigate suddenly and violently turned to starboard. It was warned off repeatedly but kept decreasing the radius of its turn. The *Dingo* took evasive maneuvers, but a collision occurred which effectively sheared off the *Dingo*'s bow. The Chinese frigate may have been damaged as well, but it sped out of the area at what looked to be full speed.

"Other vessels in the allied task force then moved in to assist the disabled *Dingo*. The *Dingo* was not in danger of sinking with its many water-tight compartments. But it was disabled and needed to be towed to port.

"As the tow was being established, two Chengdu J-20, Version 4, fighter jets took off from the concrete airstrip the Chinese military just commissioned on their new island. The jets made six, nearly supersonic, low-level passes over the stricken *Dingo* and the designated tow ship, the Australian tender *HMAS Wallaby*.

"One Chinese fighter returned to base. The other presumably thought it would make another high-speed pass, but this time over the *USS Barack Obama*. It was warned off three times quickly as it penetrated the no-fly zone, but it did not heed the warnings. It was subsequently shot down by one of the carrier's Super Hornet II fighter aircraft. It crashed into the sea less than a nautical mile from the *Obama*. The pilot went down with the wreckage of the sinking aircraft.

"China has declared that the downing of their jet was a clear act of aggression and provocation on our part. They are saying on their state media that the cold war is now over with the US, and we are into something like the so-called phony war at the start of World War Two. Our intelligence indicates they are mobilizing more ships to the area. They are also moving ten armoured divisions, two airborne divisions and a mobile missile regiment to their border with India for some reason.

"That concludes my briefing, Admiral, and other honourable members of the Joint Chiefs of Staff."

There was a prolonged silence in the room. Then the highest-ranking Marine in the room, General Vic Barnsley, growled, "It sounds like the Chinese leadership has gone completely bonkers, Rear Admiral Gammon. What is their major malfunction?"

"I have nothing new on that myself, General," Gammon replied calmy. "But the NSA has indicated their may be a struggle brewing among their top leaders."

No one else said anything, so Admiral Nichols, said, "Right, thank you Rear Admiral Gammon. It's clear to me that we need to advise the Secretary of State that we believe the President should immediately put us on DEFCON3. Quick show of hands. Against? No one. For? Everyone. Thanks people, this meeting is adjourned. And God help us all if mad fools are now running China."

25

Tommy Jenkins was a white supremacist, but he considered himself a true American patriot. He was a devoted follower of Larry Rhodes and believed everything Larry said on his radio talk shows, and at right-wing political rallies. Tommy had tried to meet Larry at rallies a few times, but he had always been turned away by security guards. Still, he was convinced Larry would be the best President the United States ever had, and he wanted to do his small little bit to help him get there.

Larry was always saying that China was behind everything that was going wrong in the US. He said that over the last three decades, China had purposely ruined the US economy as part of its warped and evil communist ideology. He said China had deliberately dumped inferior goods made by slave labour on to the US market to raise unemployment and keep wages low. He said China had created viruses that had caused murderous and devastating pandemics. He said that if climate change was really happening, which he doubted, China would be behind it because they were building more and more coal-fired electrical power plants. And now he was saying this ZONT-2 space station would just be a platform for an energy beam weapon that China would control and use to finish the job of wiping out the United States.

And Tommy believed that Chinese people were sub-human because they were not white, or Aryan as Hitler and Himmler had said. And Black people were sub-human as well, and so were Hispanic people.

Tommy inherited a small ranch in west Texas when his mother had died. He never knew his father. The two ranch hands on the farm took off when all the neighbours left because climate change had turned the region into a virtual desert. Tommy blamed China for that, because Larry Rhodes had essentially said he should on his radio talk show.

Tommy was not very bright, and he joined the US Army because they seemed to be the only people willing to hire him. He met Troy Ward during basic training. The two young men hit it off from the start. It was love at first sight, but they hid their homosexual impulses to stay in the Army without any harassment from other soldiers, or hassles from sergeants.

Troy Ward was not fanatically racist like Tommy Jenkins, but he was an extreme libertarian who enjoyed reading, creating and spreading antigovernment propaganda. Tommy was impressed when Troy told him he had shot and killed a Black man, and then a month later, a Hispanic man. Robbery had been the motive, and Troy admitted that on both occasions the pickings had been slim. There had been no witnesses. He had beat both raps by claiming his assailants had attacked him with a knife. He had thrown a knife on the ground beside each dead body. He had carefully wiped his own prints off the knives. He had also claimed that he had fired a warning shot in each murder. His Magnum 44 revolver had two empty cartridges in it when he had handed it to police on both occasions. But also on both occasions, Troy knew the warning shot had been the *second* shot. The judges had bought into his assertions of innocence and self defence and did not seem concerned at all that there were no prints of any kind on the knives found at the two crime scenes.

But the police had never bought into any of it, and they kept a close eye on Troy. He joined the Army to evade what he considered to be police harassment.

Troy was also a bit of a history buff, at least for the radical, right-wing, fringe stuff he was into. He knew all about secret government conspiracies, like the hiding of UFOs, the denial of the existence of ancient and modern day aliens, and the evil CIA and FBI people behind things like 9/11 and the assassination of John F. Kennedy. And he was a big fan of Timothy McVeigh and Terry Nichols, the famous Oklahoma City bombers of 1995. He considered both men heroes and American patriots. To Troy, no government could ever be trusted, and his personal liberties were all that mattered. He soon convinced his friend Tommy that they should emulate what McVeigh and Nichols had accomplished as soon as they could get honourably discharged from the Army.

Troy wanted to 'hurt the government bad' and get more people thinking a government-free world would be a good thing. He was not especially fussy if it was the US government or the Texas government that he hurt, as he had always struggled to understand the differences between the two.

Tommy was not too sure that he fully agreed with Troy's agenda. He wanted to 'hurt the Chinese government bad' and stop their space weapon project. He knew there were mostly Americans working in the ZONT-2 Corporation's Austin-based design facility, but he considered them all traitors.

Upon honourable discharge, the two men got married in Las Vegas and set up covert operations in Tommy's dilapidated ranch house in west Texas. They got started right away with accumulating the materials they would need for their truck bomb.

Almost like Nichols had done, they drove Tommy's inherited, ten-year-old, one-ton, Ford pick-up truck north to McPherson, Kansas. They bought enough bagged ammonium nitrate fertilizer to fill the truck. The farm supply business owner had been suspicious, as the truck was covered in confederate flag, KKK, and 'I'M A MERKAN' stickers. The two men had also made highly offensive racial jokes while the store's Black assistant manager had helped to load the truck. When Tommy proposed to pay with a credit card, the store owner asked to see a picture identification card with a farm address on it, proving the fertilizer would be used as fertilizer. Tommy initially got angry, but then Troy calmed him down, and offered to pay with cash. The shop owner accepted the cash, after looking carefully at Tommy's driver's licence, while his Black assistant manager secretly photographed the truck's licence plate number with his smart phone. When the two suspicious and offensive young men had departed the scene to the south in a dust cloud, the shop owner immediately reported the details of the transaction to the Kansas State Police

Like McVeigh, Troy had wanted to use hydrazine as another component in their bomb. But when Tommy found out the chemical was mostly made in China, he would have none of that scheme. Plus, it was very expensive. So, like McVeigh, they decided to use nitromethane instead. But you could not just go to any old store and buy nitromethane. They cased out how the Texas Motorplex received shipments of the stuff for NHRA drag races. They forced a fuel delivery truck off a lonely farm-to-market road, and Troy shot the Hispanic driver to death. He enjoyed doing that. Then they quickly transferred the drums of nitromethane to Tommy's truck and drove off.

And then they drove back to Kansas and stole tubes of explosive and electric blasting caps from a new quarry near the one that McVeigh had targeted decades before.

Troy then used his credit card to rent a two-and-a-half-ton panel truck for two days. There was not much credit left on the card, but it was enough. He drove the truck into the only barn left standing on Tommy's ranch, and the two men set to work. They mixed and packed the bomb ingredients into old, rusty, forty-two-gallon, oilfield barrels that they had stolen. They thought they had rigged a time-delayed, electrically triggered fuse that could be ignited by flicking a simple switch in the cab. But the two men did not really know what they were doing with explosives or fuses. The stuff they found on the internet was rather vague for some reason. So, they also rigged a back-up fuse that could be ignited with a blast from Troy's Magnum 44 revolver. They were pretty sure that one would work. But if they decided for some reason they just had to use that fuse, one of them at least would be destroyed by the ensuing blast.

Then the two-men used felt rollers taped to long sticks to paint the panels on the truck white, completely covering over the leasing company's logo and brand-promoting paint work. Then they applied homemade stickers to the sides of the truck with 'ACE MOVERS' in big, crooked, black letters. It was a crude job, but the truck looked like something a struggling small business owner might use.

The next day, at six o'clock in the morning on August 20, 2040, a drone controlled by the FBI discreetly watched as the two young men opened the doors on Tommy's barn. Then the drone stealthily followed behind the truck from a safe distance. Troy drove it southwards, with Tommy at his side, down a dusty gravel farm lane to the Brooks-Pecos Road. When the truck reached the 'T' intersection with the road, Troy turned it to the left or the east. The two men planned to head to the town of Toyah, then take farm-to-market and ranch-to-market backroads to Austin.

Tommy and Troy had spent the night arguing whether their target should be the Texas State Capital Building, or the four-building, PlasTekhKorp complex in Pilot Knob, a suburb just to the south of the

Austin-Bergstrom International Airport. They had finally settled on the PlasTekhKorp complex, as they thought they could park the truck, lock its doors, and leave it unoccupied on a central traffic circle to take out all four glass-clad, ten-storey buildings. In other words, they thought they could do a lot more damage and kill a lot more people by going after the PlasTekhKorp Complex.

They had left a letter on Tommy's kitchen table addressed to 'The Government' that said China had blackmailed them into doing their mega bombing deed, but ultimately the US Government was to blame by not doing enough to stop China from proceeding with their ZONT-2 space weapon. They had mailed the same letter to the *Austin Lonestar* newspaper the day before in the guise of an anonymous letter to the editor. They agreed to burn the letter on the kitchen table if they successfully pulled off and survived their first terrorist operation. And then they agreed they would go after the Texas State Capital Building next.

Troy noted there were no cars or trucks on the road. Tommy explained that was typical these days as his neighbours had all, 'bugged out' long ago. The surrounding land was flat and desert-like. The ditches were deep on both sides of the pot-holed and cracked, two-lane paved road.

Suddenly Tommy yelled, "Hey what's that, Troy? Up ahead! Look!"

Troy gradually slowed the truck down and squinted his eyes into the glare from the rising sun. Then he barked with fear in his voice, "I think it's a freaking drone, Tommy! Hovering over the centre line of the road! And it's a big one, with blue and red flashing lights!"

"Yep, the State Mounties are using them now, I heard," Tommy replied with a waver in his voice. "And they are also using nets with steel spikes. It looks like the drone is hovering over one of those nasty suckers."

"Holy crap, and there's no way I can turn around!" yelled Troy frantically. "Hang on, Tommy, I'm going to back her up!"

Troy used the side-view mirrors to back the truck up as fast as he could go without heading into a ditch. Tommy alternated between watching the stationary drone in front and looking backwards with the passenger-side mirror. After they had travelled a quarter of a mile or so, he yelled, "Troy, I see another drone behind us now, and I think it just dropped something on to the road! Geez, you know what, I think its another freaking spike net!"

Troy slowed the truck down to a stop, and mumbled, "Yes, I think you're right, Tommy. Bloody hell, it looks like we're completely screwed! They must be on to us. So, we can't go back, that's for sure. Our only chance is to go forward and make a run for it."

"Okay, Troy, let's adios, amigo!"

The truck quickly accelerated. As they approached the drone ahead of them, it simply rose upwards, while still hovering over the spike net. The truck ran over the spike net, and it came to a screeching halt as the net immediately wrapped many times around the instantly deflated front tires. The truck was still somehow upright and on the road with its nose almost in the left-hand ditch.

The two men sat in stunned silence for a long moment.

Then Tommy said, "I think this is the end of the line, Troy."

"Yes, I'm afraid so, and we know what we must do now, Tommy. Here, you can do it better from your side. The gun is in the glove box."

Tommy pulled Troy's Magnum 44 revolver out of the glove box and offered Troy his left hand. They held hands tightly. Then he said, "I love you, Troy."

"I love you too, Tommy."

They were still holding hands like Thelma and Louise when the crude, but effective, truck bomb exploded. The crack of the shock wave from the blast was heard by motorists on the I-10 interstate highway twenty miles to the south. A window blew into a ranch house eight miles to the north, injuring the sole female occupant. Her cuts from broken glass were numerous but not life threatening. Otherwise, the only casualties, other than Troy and Tommy, were two Texas State Police spike-net deploying drones, and an FBI surveillance drone.

26

As soon as he was summoned, Vice President Christos Balaskas briskly walked into the Oval Office in the White House. President Kate Winslow was alone in the voluminous room with its formal and famous furniture. She was sitting behind her huge desk and beckoned with her right hand for Christos to sit down opposite her.

Kate Winslow was fifty-five years old. She had been a Senator for two terms and had a seat in the House of Representatives before that for two terms. She was a lawyer but had spent her whole adult life involved with politics. Her husband was a practising defence lawyer and he had always been her 'advisor', which meant he had always tried to keep her grounded and value centred.

Kate was not especially pretty but she liked to be dressed up most of the time. Christos thought she used too much make-up and attributed that to a bit of insecurity about her looks. But he had great respect for his boss and would do virtually anything he could to help her out and keep her in office. They were completely aligned on most political matters.

Kate was visibly worried and anxious, and she immediately blurted out, "So, what have we found out, Chris?"

"Okay, Madam President, quite a lot, actually. First, there is no indication that China had anything to do with the massive explosion out in the sticks of west Texas. There is no money or forensic trail that would lead back to the Chinese. And there is no indication that they might have used an intermediary, mercenary group like the UPKP. And as far as we know, the UPKP currently has no operatives in the USA.

"The two suspects had just been honourably discharged from the US Army. They had been regular, short-term soldiers and they had no special training with explosives, special tactics, or special weaponry. They might have been able to glean enough information from the internet, however, to assemble a crude and powerful, so called improvised explosive device. International police forces struggle to keep up with illegal postings from terrorist groups, and some nasty and dangerous stuff slips through sometimes.

"It appears that they used their own funds to buy what they needed, or else they stole what they needed. And there was not a lot of money required for what they constructed anyway. They may have been influenced by the recent actions of the UPKP, but there is no obvious connection.

"You may recall that the UPKP immediately claimed responsibility for the explosion. They said the Texas State Police murdered their two heroes who were on their way to the next battle in the holy jihad against the ZONT-2 space weapon, and thereby made them into martyrs. But that seems to be a complete fabrication to further the UPKP's sick brand of terrorism."

"So, this is probably a case of good police work that foiled what presumably was going to be an act of domestic terrorism on a huge scale?"

"Yes, that's the consensus view. The FBI, ATF and the Texas State Police worked well together and did a fantastic job. The Texas State Police passed on a tip they received from the Kansas State Police. There was a suspicious purchase in Kansas of ammonium nitrate in fertilizer form, and, well, the two suspects were under close FBI surveillance from that point onwards, mostly using drones.

"One of the terrorists, Troy Ward, was known to police. They think he murdered two people, but they could never produce sufficient evidence to have him convicted in a court of law. He was also banned from social media for promoting anti-government hate literature. The other suspect, Tommy Jenkins, was probably just a gullible simpleton who believed everything extreme right-wing people with political agendas, like Larry Rhodes, say. His Army record indicates he was reprimanded twice for proactively sharing his racist views with his fellow white soldiers. He also once got into a fight with a Black soldier who heard some of his racist talk, and he ended up spending a week in the infirmary.

"Now, the FBI decided to wait until the two suspects made a definitive move in case a link would become apparent with other criminal or terrorist organizations. In other words, they were wondering if these two guys were being manipulated by a brainier, and more sinister, terrorist organization.

"By analysing their unusual purchases, and the huge quantities involved, and by tying those purchases to some recent unsolved thefts, the FBI thought these two amateurish characters might be making a truck bomb. And they knew their base of operations was literally out in the sticks, where they could safely attempt an arrest, or if that did not go down well and the suspects exploded their device, the damage to life and property would be minimal. It was simply a matter of choosing the right spot on a largely deserted road that they could block off in advance to protect the public. And they pulled it off, and very well I might add, with the help of the Texas State Police."

"Okay, most of that is stress relieving, and I thank you for that. But I heard a rumour that the *Austin Lonestar* newspaper stupidly and maliciously published the terrorists' incendiary, anonymous letter to the editor, without consulting with the police or with us. Is that true?"

"Yes, they did, unfortunately. China subsequently denounced any involvement with the incident and threatened further retaliatory military escalation, alleging a smear campaign by your administration. Then the FBI knocked on the right-wing Austin newspaper's door to confiscate the letter as evidence in a serious act of suspected domestic terrorism. After a few days, the newspaper printed a retraction and an apology, 'for doing something reckless and foolish'. The editor has just been suspended without pay, pending an internal review.

"And the location of the other letter, and forensic analyses, confirmed the two wannabe mass murders made their bomb in Tommy Jenkin's barn. They could do it all without help from China and the UPKP. And they had an independent motive, or at least had agreed upon one."

"Okay, so what was their target?"

"The consensus view is something government related, maybe in Austin. They were clearly emulating what the Oklahoma City bombers did back in 1995. There are distinct, irrefutable similarities. Or they might have been targeting the PlasTekhKorp Complex, which is also in Austin. The Texas government and PlasTekhKorp have been advised to increase and upgrade their security measures, and it looks like they are doing just that."

"So, we are at DEFCON3 now, and you are also suggesting there is no reason to go to DEFCON2, right?"

"Yes, I agree with the Secretary of Defence and the Joint Chiefs of Staff on this one. DEFCON2 puts us only one stupid mistake away from nuclear war with China and will put all our armed forces on edge. Heightened readiness takes a human toll, and over-worked, over-stressed people make stupid mistakes."

"Yes, I know that firsthand. So, do you think we should now do something proactive, Chris?"

"Yes, I think we should also try to calm the Chinese and their armed forces down as well. We could issue a public statement that we and our law enforcement agencies believe the two suspects acted alone, and they were domestic terrorists who were stopped in their tracks by effective, coordinated police work. We should also specifically congratulate the FBI, ATF, Kansas State Police, and the Texas State Police for a job well done. And we should assure the American people that they are safe with these competent and tireless folks out there working in the trenches and gutters on their behalf. Or something like that."

"Yes, that sounds really good. Would you draft something up with Press Secretary Mary Walker for my signature?"

"Yes, glad to do so, Madam President."

"Thanks. And why don't you ever call me Kate?"

"I do, Madam President, but never in your presence, and especially never in this holiest of holy places in America."

The President smiled, and said, "Okay, Mister Vice President. Let's proceed as discussed."

27

Nasir Abd Al-Rashid was not especially fond of Kuwait City, but he had a luxurious condo there, and he had a long-standing business relationship with a discreet pimp who helped to make his infrequent visits passably enjoyable. The pimp also provided his services to some top advisors to the Emir of Kuwait, so he was reliable, with a large, exotic stable of attractive young women and effeminate young men.

Nasir had just finished a very difficult discussion in the desert with two Chinese intelligence agents. Kuwait had been a reliable ally of China for decades, and China had funded many important infrastructure projects in the country. So, people of Chinese descent or mixed Chinese descent were not uncommon in Kuwait.

Despite decades of Chinese investment, Kuwait just could not seem to escape a crushing economic crisis. At the root of it was rampant corruption. It was everywhere, which meant there were tremendous opportunities for people like Nasir.

Nasir was wearing one of his many disguises. He was sporting a fake goatee beard, and his driver, Ahmed Badawi, was sporting a fake, bushy, untrimmed beard. Nasir had used this overall disguise before a few times, as he thought it was especially creative. The meeting with the Chinese had been near an exploration drilling wellsite lease that was under construction in the desert northwest of Kuwait City. He and his driver were dressed in working-man clothes, and dirty coveralls emblazoned with the logo of a drilling bit company. The same logo was painted on the doors of the dusty, Toyota, four-door, extended-cab, three-quarter tonne pick-up truck they were using. Nasir in fact owned the bit company, and the truck as well, but all via layers of hard to trace shell companies. There were a few boxed-up, expensive, poly-crystalline diamond compact bits, and synthetic diamond, matrix-impregnated and encrusted, coring bits, in the open, dusty box of the truck. There was also an assortment of different sized, new, and used, much cheaper, tungsten-carbide insert bits, in the back of the truck to enhance the disguise.

The two Chinese agents had angrily informed Nasir that the Chinese government was not at all happy with the recent activities of the UPKP, and by extension, with Nasir himself, as he had personally recommended their mercenary services as top class.

The indisputable fact was there had simply been too many failures. The US Deputy Secretary of State had been killed in London, but the target had been the US President. The suicide bombers in Brussels could not even get past the first barricade, and the NATO conference had proceeded as scheduled. The bombs intended for the Tel Aviv government complex could not even get off the delivery boat in Beirut harbour. The Moscow bomb had killed and terrorised a lot of people, but the PlasTekhKorp building, and its many hard to replace, highly skilled and professional occupants, had survived unscathed.

And the Chinese government was especially angered that an apparent amateurish act of domestic terrorism in the US had been linked back to them on social media through alleged and unproven funding of the UPKP. And this was all because the UPKP had arrogantly and stupidly taken credit for the botched bombing attempt! Nasir was at a complete loss to explain how that had occurred, and he acknowledged that it was personally discrediting and embarrassing.

The two Chinese agents had then been blunt with Nasir. If the upcoming Geneva job did not go exactly as planned, the services of the UPKP would be terminated. They were slightly more subtle about how perilous Nasir's situation had become. They had said, "And of course there will be consequences for you as well, and your handshake only business relationship with China."

Of course, that was the information that was most disturbing to Nasir. He knew that his many businesses would fail if his lucrative relationship with China cratered.

He had then told the two Chinese agents to relay to their masters that he would personally ensure the destruction of the Wardenclyffe complex in Geneva would occur as planned. They had seemed unimpressed by his personal assurances, but they had finally shaken hands, and the details of the next convoluted, multi-layered, money transfer were provided to

Nasir in a letter-sized envelope. The Chinese government was increasingly paranoid about all forms of electronic communication, as it feared retaliatory cyber hacking and data thefts. Nasir had to promise he would destroy the paper document just as soon as he had transferred the information it contained to his personal, un-networked, cybersecure data storage system.

After the hour-long meeting, Nasir's plan was to have Ahmed drive them back south in the bit-hauling pick-up truck on a dirt road until they got to Highway 70. Then they would turn left and take that highway back to Al Jahra and then on to his condo in Kuwait City.

Nasir had no idea how he could fulfill his guarantee that the UPKP would perform the upcoming Geneva job flawlessly. He figured he needed to clear his mind with a distraction so he could think clearly and creatively. It was now late in the afternoon, and the evening was quickly approaching. He could not decide if the evening distraction would best be a young man or young woman. Then he figured, since his mind was really muddled, maybe it should be one of each. They could sit comfortably on the back seats of the truck after they picked them up enroute to Nasir's condo. He would use his cell phone to call his pimp to arrange everything. Nasir knew Ahmed had heard lots of similar calls before and would keep his mouth shut about it.

But Nasir's perverted wool gathering, and scheming, was rudely interrupted when his driver Ahmed yelled, "Trouble ahead, boss! Looks like a Kuwait Police roadblock."

A jeep with two uniformed police officers had pulled across the narrow dirt road ahead, blocking the way. "What the hell are they doing way out here, Ahmed?' Nasir asked loudly with growing alarm. But then he remembered his many contacts in the Kuwait Police Force, and the many favours they owed him. He was calm and collected when the two police officers approached the truck, one on either side.

"Would you step out of the vehicle please?" the officer on the left said in Arabic to Ahmed through the now open driver's side window. The police officer was in fact the code-named agent Wyatt, a Shia Arab mercenary working for Mossad.

"You too, sir, step out of the vehicle, please," the other officer said to Nasir through the now open window on the passenger's side. The officer was in fact the code-named agent Virgil, a Sunni Arab mercenary also working for Mossad.

Ahmed opened the door immediately and stepped out of the truck. The officer barked, "Turn around, put your hands on the roof wide apart, and spread your legs."

Ahmed immediately complied.

Nasir refused to get out of the truck. He growled, "You fools, do you have any idea who I am?"

The officer on the right-side of the truck then drew his machine pistol and yelled, "Get out of the truck, right now!"

"Better do as he says, boss!" Ahmed yelled with a crack in his voice from the other side of the truck.

Nasir reluctantly opened the door and stepped out. The police officer yelled, "Turn around, and put your hands on the roof! Wider! Spread your legs apart too! Wider!"

The two officers then methodically searched Ahmed and Nasir from head to foot. They took their wallets and did not even look at their identification cards. The officer on the left placed Ahmed's automatic pistol on to the ground and pocketed the keys to the truck. The officer on the right carefully folded the envelope the Chinese agents had given to Nasir, put it in his shirt pocket, and re-buttoned the flap.

Then the two police officers put handcuffs on their two captives, so that their arms faced forward.

Then the officer on the right yelled, "Now, Wyatt!"

Wyatt plunged a long, sharp knife deep into Ahmed's back. He held the palm of his left hand firmly over Ahmed's mouth while twisting the knife with his right hand. Ahmed's prolonged scream of agony was still quite audible, but there was no one else around to hear it.

Virgil simply gave Nasir's head a violent twist and broke his neck instantly. Virgil was a huge brute of a man, and he had lots of practice killing men that way.

Virgil and Nasir then dragged the two fresh corpses over to their stolen police jeep and sat them down in the two front seats. They even fastened the seat belts around the corpses. They also wiped the prints off Ahmed's pistol and placed it in the back of the jeep. Then they pushed the jeep off the dirt road and into a ravine. Then they poured two full jerry cans of gasoline over the bodies and the whole interior of the jeep. They left a wide trail of gasoline back to the road and lit a match to it. The truck erupted into a black and orange fireball.

"Let's get the hell out of here, Wyatt!" Virgil yelled. "You've got the keys, so you'll drive!"

Wyatt drove the bit-delivery truck back to Kuwait City. No one seemed to think it was unusual for two uniformed Kuwait Police officers to be driving around in an oilfield service truck. It was a common enough practice, and a great way for the police to catch speeders and fetch a few bribes.

They parked the truck about three blocks from the harbour, and Wyatt threw the keys down a sewer drain. They nonchalantly walked down to the harbour, still in their stolen police uniforms, and sat down at the end of a broken-down dock. They waited there until it was pitch dark. There was no one else around. Right on cue, precisely at twenty-one-hundred hours local time, a semi-inflatable boat pulled up to the dock. The boat was powered by a quiet, electric-powered, outboard motor. It was driven by their colleague with the code name of Doc.

Wyatt and Virgil climbed into the boat and Doc drove it out to a smallish, rusty, gasoline and diesel hauling ship that was moored in the harbour. They hoisted themselves up one-by-one to stairs that had been temporarily lowered on the port side of the vessel. There was a bit of a swell and some one-metre wave action, so they had to time their jumps to securely grab on to the bottom of the stairs. Doc was the last to leave the little boat, and he kicked it away to set it adrift.

At the top of the stairs, they were greeted by Yitzchak Ben Dod of Mossad. He shook hands with the three men, and asked Virgil quietly, "How did it go?"

"Perfectly, boss. What did you expect? Oh, here's an envelope I found on Nasir. It might be something interesting."

Yitzchak laughed quietly, and replied, "Right. We're not the UPKP, are we?" Then he added in a more serious tone, "I'll look at the contents of the envelope later, in a better light. So, look, you guys, we'll all be able-bodied seamen for a while, with identification cards and passports to match. And we have safe passage to Beirut through the Suez Canal. So, let's go visit the purser, who will get you all kitted out."

28

Exclusive Report
Freeworld Press
London, UK
October 11, 2040

Freeworld Press announced today that it has uncovered indisputable evidence that China has been secretly funding, and thereby directing, the recent activities of the UPKP terrorist organization.

An undisclosed source has shared with Freeworld Press a paper copy of a document that details an elaborate, incredibly complex process for transferring money from a state-owned bank in Hong Kong to the UPKP. The final payment to the UPKP was to be in Swiss francs, presumably for UPKP's next targeted act of terrorism.

The undisclosed source also revealed that the original paper document was forwarded to the European Financial Intelligence Unit Network. The EFIUN has confirmed to Freeworld Press that the matter is now under serious investigation. The EFIUN has also directed Freeworld Press not to share its copy of the document with the public until the EFIUN investigation has been completed, and the current location of the funds in the multi-stage transfer process has been determined, and the funds secured.

The elaborate money transfer and money laundering scheme involved, among other things, five currency exchanges, two cyber currency transactions, the delivery and sale of arms to an African country that was to be paid for with actual diamonds, and the purchase of a tanker-load of crude oil at sea. In the middle of the complicated, possibly illegal, financial transaction was Nasir Abd Al-Rashid, a wealthy Middle Eastern oligarch. Mister Al-Rashid's whereabouts are currently unknown. The directors and CEOs of the many businesses he owns claim they do not know where he is either. He has apparently not been in contact with anyone for over two weeks.

Freeworld Press has contacted the Chinese Ambassador to the UN for comment. The Ambassador said, "China denies all these obviously false allegations, which China believes originated with the US government with malicious intent." Also, the Ambassador said that in the next UN Security Council meeting, China will accuse the United States of America of inciting a world war.

Furthermore, the Chinese Ambassador to the UN said China intends to sue Freeworld Press for slander, and a billion UK pounds in knock-on damages. He said he expects the suit will be filed in a British court in the next few days.

Freeworld Press stands by its statements and would welcome such a civil lawsuit if it is ever actually instigated by the Chinese government. The court proceedings would provide a legal and very public vehicle for revealing the damning document in its entirety to the free world.

29

The boyhood hero of Mustafa Faez had been Colonel Muammar Gaddafi. They had both been raised by poor Bedouin parents in the Libyan desert. They had both dreamed of a pan-Arab political union based on Sharia Law and the rather nebulous concept of Islamic Socialism. They both had wanted to lead that united Arab world as a dictator supported by a cult of personality. And they both had believed tyranny and global terrorism were the best tools to use to hold on to the power they obtained through the guise of a populist revolution.

Mustafa was now forty-nine years old. He had only been twenty years old when Gaddafi had been killed in 2011, in a most degrading manner, by the Libyan National Transitional Council. The shocking news of Gaddafi's execution had devastated Mustafa, and he had immediately gone into hiding, Bedouin-style, in the Libyan desert. He had believed he was a fugitive because he had not hidden his radical political views from anyone, nor his revolutionary political aspirations.

Mustafa became a man perpetually on the run, and he quickly became really good at it by necessity. He gradually accumulated some loyal followers, who were more a cutthroat band of murderers and thieves than a cult of personality. They survived as a gang-like organization and became relatively wealthy by raiding mostly transitional government forces in the truly messed up country of Libya.

As time passed, Mustafa realized he craved personal wealth more than power, or what he now considered to be the false utopia promised by extreme socialism. His new heroes became the oligarchs of the world, who Mustafa recognized were growing in numbers, and who were increasingly controlling the actions of world leaders behind the scenes, regardless of the way nations were politically organized.

Mustafa and his followers had been enjoying a lucrative, secret contract with the Chinese government through an Arab oligarch and agent, Nasir Abd Al-Rashid. They were aware their brand as top-flight terrorists and mercenaries had been damaged by the string of failures that had occurred. But they blamed those failures on bad luck rather than incompetence. If the money kept flowing to them, they could keep operating. But now it had suddenly stopped, and Nasir was nowhere to be found.

Mustafa was now considering approaching the Chinese government directly. But he really did not know how to do that in a covert manner that would not anger the Chinese leadership even more. Nasir had created and facilitated the Chinese connection, and it had been working so well.

China appeared to be blaming the US for everything these days, and their intense focus on the ZONT-2 space facility project seemed to have diminished. If Nasir had been found out and killed by another covert organization, Mustafa thought the Chinese government might approach him through their own intelligence agents. He figured he would make that a bit easier for them by continuing with his re-established Bedouin nomadic lifestyle, which he hoped would also make it difficult for his other enemies, both known and unknown, to find him. The logic was obviously twisted, but his followers fully bought into it. They all felt secure in the wide open, extremely hostile, Libyan-Saharan desert.

UPKP had three bases in the southern part of Libya. The facilities were mostly underground near manmade oases replenished by wells drilled into a deep aquifer. His men, and they were all men, lived in tents and moved around on camels. The mostly heterosexual men were allowed to take occasional, discreet vacations in small towns where they could use the services of female prostitutes. They were not allowed to engage in rapes, as that would bring the authorities, as incompetent as they were, down on their heads. And the few homosexual men could do whatever they wanted to, if no one saw them engaged in what the others considered to be a perverse, blasphemous act that violated Sharia Law.

Mustafa moved around with his small band of security men on camels. They had their own tents and provisions. Mustafa had a satellite phone, that was recharged by solar cells, to manage his business dealings and coordinate international UPKP activities. He always positioned his tents about two kilometres from a base. Base commanders would ride a camel out to have a face-to-face discussion with him. And Mustafa liked to move his personal camp every five days, beginning at dusk.

The UPKP agent that had been interrogated by the Mossad had told the Israeli spy organization all about Mustafa's ways, especially his logistical setup, including the location of his three underground bases in Libya. After the UPKP agent had died in a mysterious manner, Israel's Ambassador to the US had shared this logistical and organizational information with the US Secretary of State, Phyllis McMaster.

Israel clearly knew the value of this information, and as a result, had extracted a better trade agreement with the US. The CIA then shared the top-secret information with the British MI6 and the EU Intelligence Situation Centre. The CIA also let those allied intelligence agencies know that the US would be willing to work alone, 'to liquidate Mustafa and his entire Libyan organization'. It only took two days for both of those allied intelligence agencies to feed back 'off the record' that their parent governments were completely supportive of the covert American offer.

At twenty-two-hundred hours GMT on November 3, 2040, a low-orbit US spy satellite detected an electromagnetic signal coming from a tent deep within the Libyan desert. The nature of the signal corresponded to a telephone call that made use of the commercial Chinese satellite communication system. Infrared heat signatures of human beings and camels could be seen in the small tent encampment. The camp was located two kilometres from a now-known UPKP underground facility.

The information was forwarded to the Zumwalt Class II guided missile destroyer *USS Martin Luther King*. It was cruising in the Mediterranean Sea along the Libyan twelve-mile, territorial exclusion limit. An attack order was also given by US naval high command to the commander of the destroyer. The specific order was to, 'Execute Plan Sahara Fete'.

Four cruise missiles were subsequently launched from the *USS Martin Luther King* in quick succession starting at zero-two-hundred hours GMT on November 4, 2040. The missiles followed pre-programmed, ground-hugging, winding routes to their separate targets. The missiles all exploded directly over the three UPKP underground facilities, and the small camp where Mustafa Faez was sleeping. Mustafa and his bodyguards never knew what hit them.

An hour later, a fifty-year-old, perfectly functional, B-2 stealth bomber crossed into Libyan airspace. It made a completely undetected loop into and over the southern desert region of the country before departing Libyan airspace to the north. During its flight, it dropped a five ton, high-explosive, ground-penetrating, smart bomb on each of the three UPKP underground facilities, and the blackened smear on the desert where Mustafa's last camp had been located.

The Libyan government issued a formal diplomatic protest to the US government for sending four cruise missiles into its territory. It said all imports from the US would stop until a full explanation and apology was received from the US government. The US had banned its citizens from visiting Libya a decade before, so the rogue government did not have a further option of capturing and imprisoning American hostages to leverage the political response they wanted.

The US responded by saying the explanation for the attack was simple: Libya had been harbouring a known terrorist group. It also said no apology would be forthcoming, and any protests by Libya should be made to the UN Security Council.

On November 5, 2040, the Chinese representative told the other members of the UN Security Council that the US had committed an act of war, and China would help defend Libya from further acts of unprovoked aggression. China called for a vote by the Security Council to, 'condemn all the recent acts of US aggression and war mongering'. Only China voted in favour of the resolution.

30

President Kate Winslow was the last to arrive in the Situation Room. It was in the basement under the West Wing of the White House. It was a complete intelligence management centre run by National Security Council staff. In attendance were Christos Balaskas, the Vice President; Bertrand Latimore, the National Security Advisor; Susan Gilliam, the Homeland Security Advisor; and Harold Penobscot, the White House Chief of Staff. They were all sitting around a small side table where they could watch a large video screen that was controlled by supporting staff.

When the President was seated with the other VIPs at the side table, she asked with obvious concern, "So, what's going on, people?"

They all looked to Bertrand to reply to the President's question, and he immediately said, "We would like to bring up Margaret Dabrowski on the interactive screen for you, Madam President, to help answer that question. She flew to Taiwan by a military transport plane as soon as the CIA started getting wind of this new development in China. She's now in our consulate in Taipei City."

"Okay, make it so, Bert," Kate replied tersely.

Bertrand waved to a staff member at a nearby control screen, and the connection with Margaret was re-established. The top half of her body came up on the big screen. She seemed to be sitting in a large room with a lot of other people in the background who were engaged in quiet side conversations.

Bertrand said, "Hi, Margaret. Bert here again. The President has joined us now. Can you run through for us again what you think has happened?"

Margaret adjusted her professorial, wire-rimmed glasses, and replied smoothly without the use of notes, "Sure thing, Bert. Greetings, Madam President. There are a lot of similarities with this recent event and the historical arrest of the so-called Gang of Four after Mao Zedong died. It seems there was an emergency session of the twenty-five-member Political Bureau, or the Politburo for short, that sits right at the top of the leadership chart of the Chinese Communist Party. It also seems that Deng Guofeng, a member of the outer Politburo, somehow won over support from the Chinese armed forces, and he is now the President, General Secretary of the Chinese Communist Party, and Chairman of the Central Military Commission.

"We understand that the former President, Li Zheng, and three other members of the seven-member Standing Committee, or the inner Politburo, were arrested as they entered the chamber where the emergency session was to be held. The others arrested were Wang Huning, Han Yang and Zhao Zhanshu.

"Chinese media are referring to the four top people arrested as the new Gang of Four. The various media outlets are consistently saying, and I'm mostly paraphrasing, that the four, quote 'senile old men' unquote, are officially being blamed for the worst excesses during twenty-years of turmoil, the irrational and dangerous escalation of world tensions, and the failure to properly combat climate change. As soon as the arrests were made, spontaneous celebrations erupted in the streets of Beijing. And apparently, some graduate student propagandists at Beijing University were also arrested.

"Perhaps most importantly, the state media is also saying, and I'm doing a bit of paraphrasing again, that the Gang of Four's anti-revolutionary and evil plans to wield supreme power, antagonize the US and its allies into war, and eradicate the ZONT-2 project, have abruptly ended.

"We are not detecting any unusual troop movements, so Deng Guofeng may indeed have assumed and solidified full control of their armed forces. But time will tell, I suppose.

"That's about it for now."

"Wow, we didn't see this one coming," Kate replied with a grim smile. The others around the small table all nodded in agreement with her immediate reaction. "It may be a good thing, but how stable is this situation?"

"It has the outward appearance of stability, Madam President," Bertrand replied immediately. "But as Margaret just said, and most unfortunately, we will just have to wait for the real tale to become clearer over time. We don't have reliable eyes and ears within the Chinese Politburo, or within the huge city of Beijing for that matter. A lot of our intelligence is indirectly inferred from cyber hacking, the monitoring of Chinese social media, air wave monitoring, and spy satellites. We can only claim about seventy percent or so certainty at this time."

"So, we're at DEFCON3 right now," Kate observed. "What do the Secretary of Defence and the Joint Chiefs of Staff think we should do? Go to DEFCON2? Chris, I think you just talked to them, right?"

"Yes, Madam President, I did," Christos replied calmly, even though he was very stressed out. "And yes, they are recommending that we immediately go to DEFCON2. That means the whole of our armed forces must be ready to deploy and engage within six hours. The Air Force still must be ready to mobilize in fifteen minutes as established when we went to DEFCON3. If my view is worth anything, we *should* go to DEFCON2, but say publicly that we are only doing so until the new leadership in China can provide assurances to us that the country is stable and fully within their control."

"Your view is worth a lot, Chris, and I thank you for it," Kate replied sincerely. "Anyone object to what Chris just suggested?"

Susan Gilliam, the Homeland Security Advisor replied, "I agree with Chris, Madam President. But I think we also need to provide our own assurances to the American people, and the members of our armed forces, that we believe we are just being extra cautious. In other words, we should clearly let our citizens know that we do not believe we have moved closer to world war, and we will stand down again a notch or two when we confirm the situation is at least no worse than before, or hopefully, improved from a security-of-the-world point of view."

"I agree with that as well, thanks, Susan," Kate replied crisply. "Anyone else?"

Harold Penobscot, the White House Chief of Staff, then replied, "I agree with Chris and Susan, too, Madam President. In addition, I think we should get a slot for you on prime-time national television tomorrow evening where you can deliver a direct message to the American people. And I don't think we should allow any questions from the press after your statement. We need to control the message very carefully and avoid any possibilities of distortion. The Chinese government will no doubt be closely monitoring your statement as well."

"Thanks, Harold, great suggestion," Kate replied. "Please work with Press Secretary Mary Walker to write something up for my consideration.

"So, anything else I need to know about right now? No? Great, so, we will proceed along those lines, then. Please call me back down here again any time you think it is necessary. Thanks everyone."

31

On December 14, 2040, a cybersecure videoconference link was established between the three CEOs behind the ZONT-2 project: Timofey Semenov, Alain Dufort and Holt Carson. Once again, they established the link themselves to add an extra level of security. They were all still a bit clumsy with the multiple passwords, and the voice, retina, and face recognition bits, so it took a little longer than they had hoped for to get connected.

Alain was the first to say something when everyone's face popped up on a computer screen that was split into three vertical panels. "Hey there, Tim, and Holt! Not getting any easier, is it?"

"No, Alain, but it's still critically necessary, unfortunately," Timofey replied with a bit of angst. "It seems to me our list of detractors and outright enemies does not seem to be getting any smaller. But I hope you two guys might have a different perspective. We clearly need to talk about our situation, openly and realistically. Holt, I think Alain and I would greatly benefit if you quickly ran through where *you* think we are with the ZONT-2 project. From my angle, progress seems to be convoluted and confusing, and perhaps stalled."

"Yes, I'm sorry to say it is, guys, and the coup in China has muddled the already murky puddle for sure," Holt replied with a shake of his head. "But I urge you to try not to be too despondent or too cynical, Tim, at least with people outside of our little group. My old man used to say, 'Where there's manure, Holt, there's opportunity'. Now, he owned a ranch, and he really *was* talking about manure fertilizer. But still, the shocking development in China may present us with an opportunity, too. I hope we can get into that possibility in a few minutes.

"As you know, we're now all happy with the Basis of Design document, and here in Austin we are well into the detailed design phase, even though we do not have a Memorandum of Understanding yet with even *one* country.

"Technically, the project now looks immensely doable, but we have encountered some manufacturing and structural member extrusion process struggles along the way. We have settled on eight different types of structural elements. They are of various lengths, but they average about ten metres long. The eight element types, or building blocks, are fitted together to form the integrated structure. There are also small plus-sign shaped pieces to form the square, grid intersections.

"I suppose the structure is rather like a giant DNA molecule, except it is planar and not a double helix. There are only four nitrogenous bases in DNA, plus phosphate and a type of sugar. And it is the sequencing of the four bases within the massive DNA molecule that determine the unique characteristics of an animal life form on the Earth. In contrast, our eight types of structural elements are usually located in the same places around a one-hundred-metre per side square cell. And the replicated cells form our rigid, umbrella-supporting structure.

"We just could not figure out a way to manufacture two of the eight structural element types without unacceptable distortion. However, a Canadian ex-pat, carbon-fibre, process engineer in PlasTekhKorp's California plant came up with an elegant, remarkable, and patentable solution for us. We have trialled his new process in a zero-G environment in ALINA-1, and I am extremely pleased to say there was perfect repeatability and perfect, thermally stable, dimensional specs.

"Project-approval-wise, we have not passed through the first decision gate. Our business model calls for the decision makers at every gate to be the ones paying the capital costs. So, basically, we are just spinning our wheels, and spending your money, until we know who we are trying to please.

"Also, as you know, our own preferred concept of Stage One is a square structure that is ten kilometres by ten kilometres in size. When completed, it would be able to beam seven-hundred and fifty megawatts of power to the Earth, twenty-four hours a day, year-round.

"Thirty-five countries have been at least willing to talk to us. The big hold out has been China, who has completely shut us out, and we believe literally tried to blow us all up. And at the same time, China has tried to intimidate and frighten the dickens out of the entire world with pseudo-Islamic terror attacks conducted by UPKP mercenaries.

"But the EU and the US have been especially difficult to deal with as well. They have their own internal political squabbles that never seem to end. And I guess in line with historical precedent, the biggest world powers are paranoid about literally any other country getting the upper hand.

"Recently, in our negotiations, we have been throwing out a trial balloon that Alain suggested after he first talked to Mei Wu-Toussaint, a person with secret insight into what happens inside the Chinese Politburo. This trial balloon is the notion that the CEO of the joint venture corporation, or yours truly, could report to, and work for, a board of directors with appointed representatives from twelve countries, or groups of countries. Specifically, we've been talking about Canada, the USA, Brazil, Argentina, the UK, the EU countries in aggregate, South Africa, Saudi Arabia, Russia, China, India and Australia. By treaty, these parties would also have to actively consult with other countries in defined regions, and they would have to agree, I guess by treaty again, to vote on board matters according to the majority consensus in each region.

"Surprisingly, no one we have been talking to has completely rejected this idea, and it may even be starting to get some traction. Everyone agrees that we can never proceed without an authorizing resolution by the UN General Assembly. That means fifty percent of the countries in the world must be in favour of the resolution, plus at least one vote. The resolution will basically be a new, overriding space law. And if our proposal remains to run ZONT-2 as a private venture, most countries believe we will never get China, the US and all of the EU nations to come onboard with us. And those are the folks with the biggest pockets full of cash to help us, and on the negative side and metaphorically again, the biggest piles of rocks to throw at us to hurt us.

"The business model that seems to be tentatively agreeable to the thirty-five interested countries is that of a regulated utility, owned by investing countries, regulated by the UN, with governance provided by the twelve-member board of directors. And the thirty-five interested countries mostly agree that Wardenclyffe and PlasTekhKorp should be the prime service providers to the joint venture corporation for a defined, first stage of the project. They see this as a just reward for initiating this potentially world-saving venture, and fair compensation for the ZONT-

1 pilot project sunk costs, and for designing and advancing the ZONT-2 facility with our own, or rather your own, money.

"I know this next observation, or subjective opinion rather, might not be worth much to you two guys. But it appears to me the countries most interested in our concept of Stage One appear to be Saudi Arabia and Australia. They have large tracts of deserts, of course, and the highly unlikely, worst-case scenario of a high-intensity, microwave energy beam straying off a ground-based receiving target does not seem to bother them all that much.

"Also, I had an interesting chat with US Vice President Balaskas at a political social function last week here in Austin. It was just a Washington-style cocktail party, I suppose, but I understand that's where a lot of deal making happens within the federal government. Anyway, he told me, off the record, that he and President Winslow are big fans of our concept. Furthermore, they believe a lot of political points can be scored if Los Alamos, New Mexico is selected as one of the Stage One power receiving ground stations.

"I agree that it would be both ironic and highly uplifting if the site of the first nuclear bomb blast could be turned into something good, and the first step to a greener, healthier, and possibly more peaceful world.

"But the White House administration is apparently frustrated by the current political, domestic reality. The US is as polarized as ever, with unyielding factions within the President's own blue party. And of course, the House is blue, but the Senate is red, and that means lots of stalemates when it comes to trying to pass legislation. Now, the upcoming mid-term elections might change the currently negative outlook if Congress went completely blue. I'll come back to that one, as it might form a part of our forward strategy.

"The thirty-five tentatively amenable countries also like the idea that competitive bidding for the two primary service contracts will occur before the next or subsequent construction stage is approved. But can you guys live with that caveat? Their argument is, if we all do a good job with the Stage One construction project, your corporations would be best positioned to win the next bidding round. And your firms would stand to make a lot of money in *any* stage of the project, especially if a stage required multiple years to complete."

There was an awkward pause, but finally Timofey said, "I don't see any other way forward, Alain and Holt, than to agree to this fundamental change to our proposed business model. And I want this project to move forward, now more than ever."

Alain hesitated a while longer with his head down. Then he looked up and said, "Reluctantly, I agree with you, Tim. My ego, and greed I suppose, tell me we're giving up *way* too much. But I recognize now that the ultimate prize of total, unfettered control was somewhere between naïve and a complete fantasy. The world, with its hundreds of countries and competing factions, just does not function in a way that would allow us to operate independently, and unregulated.

"So, Holt, I think you are about to suggest we focus our immediate attention on winning over China and the US? And maybe the EU nations, too?"

Holt was silent for a few moments, and then he said confidently, "I think China and the US are the key for us. If we win them over, with their immense trading power and military might, I believe they can cajole the EU countries into coming on board too. The other thirty-five countries should be elated when they see China and the US have come on board. And then they can *all* work together to cajole at least a fifty percent majority of the UN General Assembly member countries to authorize the project."

There was another prolonged pause, then Timofey said, "You know, I may have a way to open the door for us with China. There's a rumour that the new Chinese Ambassador to Russia will be Yuhang Jintao. He was in my mechanical engineering class at Moscow Polytechnic University. We hung out with different crowds, but I had a few good chats with him. He struck me as empathic, open-minded, and pragmatic, which is not at all typical of a member of the current Chinese Communist Party. I think he will remember me, and I may be able to arrange a one-on-one discussion with him here in Moscow. It might not lead anywhere, but I am at a loss to suggest anything else."

"No, that sounds good, Tim, at least notionally," Alain replied. "Mei Wu-Toussaint is probably another primary resource for us, as she told us in advance that this coup was coming. She also suggested a way forward with our business model, that we basically just discussed, that might be agreeable to some of the folks now running China. As much as I like talking to her, I think I will ask her to talk to you directly, Tim, and help you out, if she's willing. And then you can manage the Chinese file for us point forward."

"Okay, Alain, I'll do that. So, you and Holt will manage the US file then?"

"No, I think we're going to have to crawl in the gutter to get anywhere in the US," Alain replied with a grimace. "We first need to sway popular opinion to obtain enough of the Congressional support we need. I think Holt will agree with my perception, based on my own research, and years of trying to do complicated, politically sensitive, deals in the US.

"The negative popular opinion against us is held by the one-third-plus, so called base of the red party. They are a far-right wing, largely illiterate, science-denying bunch of folks that are colloquially called rednecks. They distrust all blue governments and believe in conspiracy theories promoted on a few ultra-right-wing television and internet networks. That might present us with an opportunity, albeit an underhanded one. US politics is dirty business, and that's where I have lived most of my life. I think we need to keep Holt completely out of it. We have to be able to hold him up as the golden-haired boy who will lead us to the promised land when Stage One is sanctioned."

"Okay, my hair is brown and thinning, but I get your drift," Holt said with a smirk.

"We already agreed, Alain, that you would handle things if shall we say, unethical, or somewhat dubious, tactics were found to be required," Timofey replied carefully. "But can I observe that you have been nothing but a gentleman in our dealings together? And can I add that I truly enjoy your company, and observe again that you seem to have mellowed from the cold-hearted persona you used to project?"

"Ditto from my perspective," Holt interjected. Then he quickly added a bit sheepishly, "Boss."

There was another prolonged pause, then Alain said with a smile, "Well, I thank you both for those positive observations. I guess I *have* mellowed a bit, and made a few real friends recently in Mei, and Emma Baumgartner, and I like to think of you two guys as my friends as well.

But I can put on the old mantle of manipulation and deceit once more, I believe, since it is necessary. And I really want this project to move forward like you do, Tim and Holt… now more than ever."

32

On January 21, 2041, Timofey Semenov was escorted by an armed guard in a Chinese military uniform. The personal escort started at an intimidating security barrier directly behind the front reception desk of the Chinese Embassy in Moscow. They passed through three more security check points enroute to the office of the Chinese Ambassador to Russia. There were armed guards standing or sitting outside virtually every door in the maze-like complex.

When they finally seemed to have arrived at their destination, Timofey's guard sharply rapped on an unmarked, closed door. There was no chair or desk outside the door. A few loud words were exchanged in Mandarin with someone in the room, who Timofey assumed was the Ambassador. Then the guard opened the door, stood at attention while Timofey entered the room, and then re-closed the solid, wooden door. Timofey hoped the guard would be allowed to stand at ease outside the door.

Yuhang Jintao remained seated at his large, modern, stylish and cluttered desk, while taking a close look at his visitor. Then he smiled, rose to his feet, walked around his desk, and said pleasantly in Russian with a refined Muscovite accent, "It really *is* you, Timofey Mikhailovich. And after all these years! My word, this is joyful!"

Timofey returned the smile with a bit of relief, and the two men shook hands vigorously. Timofey had worried that he might not have been remembered by the new Ambassador. The Ambassador motioned with his right hand that Timofey should sit down on a deeply cushioned leather chair facing the left side of his desk. The Ambassador then sat down again on the modern, orthopedic, office chair behind his desk, swiveled it around, and moved it closer to face Timofey.

Timofey was immediately struck by the contrast of this office with Alain Dufort's description of the Chinese Ambassador's office in Bern, Switzerland, which Alain had visited with the top Swiss intelligence agent. The walls of this office were covered with beautifully framed photographs of famous landmarks in China, including the Great Wall. There was an elegant, free-standing, perfectly lacquered, shiny, black wooden cabinet filled with mementos from an obviously storied diplomatic career, and photographs of what Timofey concluded must be the Ambassador's close family members. In front of the wall directly behind the Ambassador's desk, a Russian flag and a Chinese flag formed an 'X' with their crossed wooden staffs, symbolically suggesting a friendly rather than an adversarial relationship between the two nations. And there were living plants all around the room, and some were quite exotic looking.

Ambassador Jintao appeared to be in top physical condition. He was a tall, wiry man, and Timofey perceived that he had aged well. He had a full head of completely black hair and a healthy, tanned complexion. And he was wearing a pair of thick, rimless glasses that made his eyes appear monstrous in size.

"It is wonderful to see you again," Timofey said sincerely. "And you look great, Mister Ambassador. Where did you get your tan?"

"My last posting was in Singapore," Jintao replied pleasantly. "And please, Timofey, call me Yuhang. We are old acquaintances and school chums, after all."

"Thank you, Yuhang, I will. So, you went from Singapore to Moscow. It must have been tough to leave a tropical paradise?"

"I liked it there, but I was only an adjutant. This is a far more important posting."

"Yes, a tremendously important job, no doubt. You must have impressed some very important people along the way."

"Perhaps, but it was more likely that I guessed right and backed the people who arrested the latest Gang of Four and who are now leading China to a better place. Now, Timofey, I would be sincerely flattered if you are just making a social call today. But I suspect there is something else on your mind."

"Yes, there are a couple of things, actually. But I hope we can reminisce a bit too before my allotted time runs out. First, have you been following the ZONT-2 project, and are you aware of my intimate involvement with it?"

"Yes, to both questions. And I am also aware that you have recently modified your proposed business model. I can relay to you and to your executive colleagues that our new leaders are intrigued by the notion of a utility, owned by contributing nations, regulated by the UN, and governed by a twelve-person board of directors. They are not agreeable, however, to some of the proposed countries who would appoint those board members. They would like to see Canada replaced by Vietnam, Argentina replaced by the Democratic Republic of the Congo, South Africa replaced by Cuba and Saudi Arabia replaced by Kuwait."

"Well, what you say encourages me to a great extent. We have frankly failed to initiate any form of dialogue with China. Would China be willing to negotiate with us about the make-up of the board of directors? You see, other countries have proposed alternatives as well, and there are multiple viewpoints."

"Yes, I believe everything is negotiable. The new China will be more business-friendly, and less isolationist. But significant changes, especially cultural changes, take time to implement. We will be asking our friends, and traditional opponents and competitors, to be patient with us while we fully work through our transition."

"I can safely say on behalf of my business partner and our project CEO that we will be patient. But does the new China feel, as we do, that the need to combat climate change is more urgent than ever?"

Yuhang paused for a moment. Then he said, "Yes, I believe so. I for one certainly feel the need for urgent proactivity. Now, Timofey, I'm surprised you have not asked how we know so much about your revised pitch to get ZONT-2 literally off the ground."

"I assumed the new China has retained the same efficient intelligence service as the old China."

"It has, but I was instructed to inform you that Mei Wu-Toussaint is a Chinese intelligence agent."

"Really? She told us she is not a communist."

"She is not a member of the Chinese Communist Party. But that is about to change. You see, you will be negotiating with her from now on. She will be on our side, not yours. Does that upset you?"

"No, but it does surprise me. And it will probably upset my colleague, Alain Dufort. He considers Mei to be a close friend. And I'm suddenly wondering if your posting to Moscow might have been planned to facilitate the delivery of a direct message to me and Mister Dufort. Perhaps you knew I would be calling on you because of our past acquaintance?"

"I would like to think my promotion was based purely on merit, but I know it was not. We needed to find a way to initiate dialogue, on our terms, without attracting attention. I suppose it is sort of a face-saving measure. There are still factions within the Chinese Communist Party that fear and distrust all other countries, and foreign-owned, capitalistic corporations. For now, we have achieved some form of stability, but we must walk warily, and look behind us at all times."

"Your metaphor is effective. I understand what you are saying. And we will be discreet."

"That is good. Now, we understand you are having similar difficulties getting traction with the US and the EU. Is that correct?"

"Yes. But we think it would really improve our negotiating power with them if we first could execute a Memorandum of Understanding with China. In addition, we now have thirty-five other countries who would come along, we believe, and contribute capital funding for a stake in the revenue and or in-kind electrical energy, with such a document in place.

"It might just be a simple case of having to basically shame the EU and US into seeing the light, so to speak. And of course, continuing with our strategy of underscoring, in every which way we can, the immense value of both a space umbrella and a totally green, money making, uninterruptable, power supply."

"Yes, I can see the logic in what you say. Now, for your information, the new China would like to strengthen the role and prestige of the UN. The world has come far too close to another nuclear conflagration. ZONT-2 could help bring nations closer together, if the business model is structured in the right way, and the operation of the facility is regulated properly and objectively. But we think building 'trust but verify' mechanisms into the final agreements or treaties, with or between nations, will be absolutely necessary."

Timofey chuckled, and said, "I believe an American President used words like 'trust but verify' to lobby for a strategic arms agreement with the Union of Soviet Socialist Republics."

"Yes, I believe you are right. But a good idea is a good idea, is it not?"

"Yes, I agree, it is."

"Now, unfortunately, I have another matter to attend to in a few minutes, Timofey. But you mentioned a second point of discussion?"

"Yes, and it seems I am never given enough time for it. You see, I am also a champion for global biodynamic farming, and…"

"And you would like an opportunity to make some inroads into China," Yuhang interjected.

"Yes, that is it exactly, Yuhang."

"Well, I was also directed to invite you to talk with Mei Wu-Toussaint about that matter, too. You see, China has always permitted and experimented with organic farming, mostly because it eliminates or greatly reduces the need for water, soil and food polluting pesticides, herbicides and fertilizers. But Chinese farms are essentially industrial, collectivized farms. The new China wants to reverse some of the extreme measures that were used to industrialize the country since the Great Revolution. Our cities, both old and new, are highly polluted and frankly, sad places, full of unhappy and unhealthy people. And unhappy people can become counterrevolutionaries.

"We want to move a lot of people back on to farms. And we want them to stay there and be happy in their work, perhaps in a traditionally peasant, or more independent, sort of way. That part is more contentious. But if we could indeed find a way, within our form of communism, to somehow establish a sort of bond, or spiritual attachment with the land, and its part in the global ecosystem, and even the cosmos, that might be desirable.

"China is officially atheistic, but people crave magical potions and elixirs. I use the word magic because there is no science behind certain beliefs in Chinese folklore. But our folklore is so powerful that entire species have been wiped out because of an insatiable desire for a particular ingredient, like a ground-up animal horn. Now, I've read that

Rudolf Steiner was not a scientist, rather a philosopher and a bit of a mystic. Is that right?"

"That is a bit too simplistic, but yes, he has been labelled as such."

"And farms must apply, using prescribed methods, nine of Steiner's so-called preparations to be certified as biodynamic, among other rigidly defined parameters?"

"Yes, that is correct."

"Okay, here is the pertinent point. Whatever we promote in China must be perceived as Chinese, and something conceived of by the Chinese Communist Party, or perhaps rediscovered by the party after years of research into ancient Chinese folklore. And it must be regulated by the Chinese government, not by Demeter or a nebulous, international group of biodynamic farmers."

"I take issue with the word 'nebulous', but please go on."

"So, our question is, would you be willing to help us develop a Chinese form of biodynamic farming, one that meets the essence of what is done elsewhere? In other words, could you live with China requiring, say, *eleven* Mao Zedong preparations for certification, if nine of them were actually, and secretly, Steiner's inventions?"

Timofey was getting a bit angry with Yuhang's linear and manipulative line of questioning. But he took a deep breath, smiled, and said, "Perhaps. Yes, I think I could live with such a compromise, Yuhang, as I believe transforming farming in China into something self-sustaining, Earth-friendly, better nourishing and spiritually fulfilling would go a long way towards solving China's problems, and by extension, the world's problems."

Yuhang then smiled, and said, "Then please, Timofey Mikhailovich, we invite you to discuss this matter as well with Mei Wu-Toussaint.

"And I am genuinely sorry that I must end our discussion now to pursue this other pressing matter I mentioned. I was greatly looking forward to a bit of reminiscing with you. My memories of my university days have faded, but I remember the overall experience fondly."

"Then perhaps we can chat another time? Say at one of the embassy functions, maybe?"

"Yes, for sure. Or, why don't you just try to book a time with my assistant? Please do not say the agenda is reminiscing, however. I will have to at least appear to be working to keep this job."

Timofey laughed, and then asked in a serious tone, "Will your assistant be one of the guards out there? The front-desk of the Embassy is staffed by people wearing what look to be Army uniforms, the same as your security guards are wearing."

Yuhang suddenly looked sad. He replied, "Yes, that is very observant, they are in fact Army uniforms, and everyone in this building other than me has just been enlisted in the Army. We are all under strict orders, however, including myself. The militarization is mostly illusory, as you cannot just tell someone they are suddenly a soldier without proper training and indoctrination. I hope this might just be a transitionary sort of thing, perhaps to give the appearance of newfound strength in a world filled with perceived threats."

"I see. Then, I will not read much into it. Well, I sincerely thank you for your time, Yuhang, and Mister Ambassador. I found our discussion to have been both illuminating and most interesting. I hope dealing with your next matter brings the same reward to you."

"It probably will not but thank you so much for the kind thought. I hope you have a good day, Timofey Mikhailovich. And it was great chatting with you again."

33

Javon Donovan was an honourably discharged, US Marine Lance Corporal, as well as a former motorcycle city cop. He had finished his civilian second career as a homicide detective with the Austin, Texas police force, and he had just retired with a stellar, completely unblemished employment record. He was sixty-three years old, Black, street-smart, and still in great shape. He was obviously muscular and only a fool would mess with him.

Javon decided he would try his hand as a private investigator. His Marine and police pensions were all right, but he figured he should endeavour to salt away some more dough before he really had to retire. He was a widower and the grandfather of two young kids, so the extra money would not just benefit himself.

He was sitting behind his third-hand desk inside a bankrupted massage parlour in the middle of a run-down strip mall in Austin, when an obviously foreign, white lady walked in. She had tried to dress casually, American style, but she still looked completely out of place. Her make-up was perfect, and her jewellery was way too upscale. She said she was working for another lady who was in turn working for a very rich and powerful person. But she said she did not want to reveal anyone's name, even her own, because of what she called, 'political sensitivities'.

Javon had replied, "Okay, ma'am, but please be advised that my services will cost a lot more that way." The lady had simply shrugged and then asked what his 'modified fees' would be. After Javon told her, she had said she would pay triple that, all in cash. And if the work she wanted Javon to do eventually led to a conviction, she said there would be a twenty-thousand-dollar cash bonus in it for him.

Javon figured anyone throwing that kind of money around was up to no good. So, he had asked her with a bit of a sneer, "What's really going on here, lady?"

The elegant but dressed-down lady had then told Javon what the job was, and who she wanted to see convicted. Javon instantly agreed it was politically sensitive. But he knew a few things about the targeted individual from his many years on the police force, often in the gutter with the rats and the other dregs of humanity, and he immediately agreed to take on the job.

After the nice foreign lady had left Javon's office, he looked at the cash retainer fee in his hand, and thought to himself, 'Hell, I'd do this one for nothing. I hate that SOB.'

Javon had always been a professional, as a soldier, a cop, and a detective. So, he first invested in thorough research about the targeted individual. He read lots of things, mostly on the internet, and talked to his buddies on the Austin police force, and his many street contacts. When he was ready, he started following the target around. He knew how to do that very stealthily. The work was boring and tedious, but Javon had arrested lots of truly bad and dangerous people after putting in some incredibly long hours on stakeouts. He knew it was often worth it.

It was quickly obvious that the rumours were right, and the target did indeed have a gambling addiction. He was not stupid enough to drink and drive while intoxicated, but whenever he won a bit of money, which was not very often, he would buy a bottle of bourbon, pick up a street hooker and head for the same cheap motel in midtown Austin off the I-35. Javon found out from a street contact that the motel manager owed the targeted individual a few favours for helping him to get his managerial job, and to help his teenage daughter get an abortion. So, the motel manager only charged the targeted individual half-rate. And he always gave the target the best room, which was a sort of suite that was far away from the motel office and reception.

After five weeks of methodically staking-out the individual, Javon noted a significant change one especially hot and humid afternoon. The target came out of his favourite casino, stumbling a bit in the bright light. He was laughing and yelling at people like he always did when he was ahead with cash. He got in his car and drove to his favourite liquor store. He came out with a quart-sized bottle of booze in a brown paper bag. Then he got back in his car and headed over to the sleazy strip where one so inclined could find a hooker at any time of the day or night.

But Javon knew there would be no hookers on this street for a few days and nights to come. The cops had successfully arrested three pimps and their harems of painted, dolled-up girls the night before.

In obvious frustration, the targeted individual then drove around to other parts of the city, but Javon knew they were only night spots for hookers.

Then the target parked his car on a suburban sideroad, and Javon watched him take a couple of long swigs from his whisky bottle. It had probably not been enough to get the target drunk, but enough for him to get a bit of a buzz on, and for any lingering inhibitions to vaporize.

Then the target drove his car over to another suburban part of town. A thunderstorm had been building, and the sky now suddenly looked threatening. The target parked his car across the street from a high school. As rambunctious and preppy kids started streaming out of the school after the closing bell, the target rolled his window down and was obviously looking for someone. After a few minutes, he yelled and waved at an attractive, blonde-haired girl who was walking quickly down the sidewalk on her own. The girl stopped for a few moments, stared at the target, then put her head down, and kept walking.

The target then followed the girl slowly along in his car, while talking to her loudly. Javon could not hear what he was saying, but he could guess what it was. The girl was obviously trying to ignore the target, but suddenly there was a flash of lightning, and a heavy downpour of white rain. The girl then saw the road was free of traffic and ran across the road to the sidewalk side of the target's car. She hurriedly climbed in on the passenger's side, and the target drove off with the girl at his side.

Javon then used his cell phone to alert a friend of his on the Austin police force about what he thought was about to go down.

He then discreetly followed the target's car. As Javon had suspected, it pulled into the parking lot of the cheap midtown motel. The target must have already booked his favourite room. He used a key to open the door. The girl was obviously hesitant to follow him into the room, but it was still raining, and she suddenly decided to run from the car to the room. The target followed her into the room with his brown paper bag in his left hand and closed the door.

Javon then saw a police cruiser with two cops in it slowly rolling along beside the motel. The cruiser had obviously arrived on the scene using a back lane. He motioned for the two officers in the car to move closer with their vehicle and follow him while he approached the target's room on foot. The cruiser stopped behind the target's parked car, and the two officers got out, one with a shotgun and the other with a drawn police revolver. Then they stood beside Javon at the door to the room and listened.

When they heard the girl scream, the officer with his revolver drawn instantly kicked the door open. Then the officer with the sergeant stripes and the shotgun barged into the room and yelled, "Freeze! This is the police!" His one-stripe partner followed behind him into the room, and Javon waited outside the door.

The target had a tight hold of the girl's naked shoulders and had obviously just ripped off her blouse. She stopped screaming and looked stunned as well as frightened.

"Let go of the girl and put your hands against the wall!" yelled the officer with the shotgun.

When the target had complied with the order, the other officer put his gun back in its holster and thoroughly searched the target. Then he said, "He's clean, Roger." Then he told the target to show him some form of identification. The target pulled out his wallet, and then he pulled out and handed over to the officer his driver's licence. He started to look angry now and no longer startled or scared. He barked, "Yeah, that's right, bubba, I'm Larry Rhodes, and I've got lots of friends on the force, in high places. Freaking right I do, bubba."

The officer replied sternly, "I'm Constable Cody Harkins, not bubba. Don't ever forget that." Then Constable Harkins put handcuffs on Larry Rhodes and pushed him back hard against the wall. "Don't move," he ordered. Then he went into the bathroom, returned with a big bath towel, and handed it to the girl. She was shaking now and weeping a bit. Then the Constable said, "Sorry, but your blouse is destroyed, miss, so please wrap yourself in this. That's better. Here, why don't you have a seat in this chair? Now, I know you just had a terrible shock, and you're still a bit scared, but here's my badge. See? I am a police officer. And so is my partner, Sergeant Roger Little. You're safe now. So, what's your name?"

"Cheryl."

"Cheryl what? What's your last name?"

"Cheryl Thomas."

"Thanks. Hold old are you, Cheryl?"

"Fourteen."

"And do you know this man, Cheryl?"

"He's... he's, my father! My *own father*!" Then she started sobbing uncontrollably, and Constable Harkins patted her towel-wrapped shoulder in sympathy.

"Is that right, Larry, this is your own daughter?" asked Sergeant Little loudly with disgust. He still had his shotgun pointed directly at Larry's chest.

"I don't have to say anything to a couple of loser cop, pecker heads," growled Larry.

Javon stuck his head in the door, and said calmly, "You'll find there is a restraining order against Larry Rhodes. He is not supposed to be anywhere near his first ex-wife and her daughter."

"Thanks, Javon," Sergeant Little replied. "Did you know your father was supposed to stay away from you, Cheryl?

"Yes," she sobbed. "I'm sorry!"

"So, why did you get into his car?"

"It was raining, and so hard, too." Talking seemed to be helping to calm her down a bit.

"Okay, and why did you come into this motel room with him?"

"He said I could meet his friend, Beau Blaze."

"The famous bull rider?"

"Yes."

"And he wasn't here, was he?"

"No. He fooled me."

"Everyone makes mistakes, Cheryl. Smart people learn from them. Read him his rights, now, Cody."

"Larry Rhodes, you are under-arrest for kidnapping, assault, attempted rape, molesting a minor and failing to obey a restraining order. You have the right to remain silent. Anything you say can and will be held against you. You have the right to an attorney…"

34

They were known as the American Gang of Four. In fact, they proudly talked about themselves that way. They were all in their second terms as members of the US House of Representatives. And they all wanted to be US Senators, because outside of the presidency, they knew that the Senate was where the real power was in America, and where the real money was, in a still wealthy, powerful and increasingly corrupt nation.

Jim Garfield considered himself the leader of the gang. He was a former high school geography and physical education teacher in a large town in Virginia. He considered himself a bit of a jock. His glory years had been in high school, where he had been renowned as a head-hunting football line backer. He had loved to spear defenceless quarterbacks with his helmet, and he had been suspended three times for those dangerous infractions. But in his adult years, he was not a very good coach, or teacher, and he had been warned twice by classroom inspectors to 'pull up his socks' as they rated him well below average.

And when there was a report that Jim Garfield had shown unusual and unwanted affection for one of the boys he coached on the football team, the head coach had told him, "You had better bugger off right now, funny boy, before we call the cops on you."

Jim then decided to run for mayor of his hometown. The other candidate was an older, nerdish kind of man, and a left-leaning academic with little popular appeal, while Jim catered to red-meat-eating conservatives and the more right-wing base of the red party. He won by a slim margin in an historically blue party and blue-collar town.

Jim had grown up hating people of colour. His parents and close friends had been bigoted that way. He reinstituted zoning laws to keep neighbourhoods, schools and businesses white in the more affluent areas of the town. The notion of district gerrymandering for political advantage came naturally to him. He then worked in a leadership role within the red party, and successfully helped it to gerrymander more favourable districts in the western part of his home state of Virginia. Then he ran for the House in one of those new districts and won rather handily.

Jim had idolized Larry Rhodes and figured he would ride his coattails right to the top of the red party. If Larry became the US President, Jim thought maybe Larry would make him his Vice President. Larry egged him on and used him for political advantage with the party's redneck base. But Larry thought Jim was a bit strange, and potentially a future liability, so he had kept him at arm's length. When Larry was arrested and convicted, that was the end of Larry's political career. And Jim Garfield thought his political dreams had also gone up in smoke.

But Jim soon saw an opportunity to join up with three other outspoken and ambitious, extreme right-wing members in the House. And Jim set his new sights on a Virginia, US Senate seat.

***

Vicky Armstrong was a former hairdresser. She was pretty good at it and started up her own business. It was successful, and she managed to turn it into a chain of hairdressing salons in her south-eastern state of Georgia. The salons were all in white, affluent neighbourhoods, where people just knew, in spite of segregation laws, that Blacks, Asians, Hispanics and Native people were not welcome. At political but social get-togethers and fundraisers, she would openly tell her new friends that those 'off-white' people could cut your grass and clean your pool, but at supper time, they had better be gone from your neighbourhood, or else. If she was drinking red wine and smoking weed at the same time, she sometimes expanded upon what she meant by 'or else'. But she always forgot about what she had said the next day. And she, too, had decided to run for Congress in a freshly gerrymandered district, and she too had won.

***

Frank Strange had started out his adult life as a mechanic who worked on farm equipment in the midwestern state of Iowa. He inherited some money from his mother. She had been a libertarian and an anti-vaxxer, and ironically and not surprisingly, she had died while she was in her mid-forties during a pandemic. Frank's wealthy, businessman father was a significant donor to the red party, and he had died in a vehicle accident when Frank was only three years old. He had been prior convicted of drunk driving three times, and the autopsy had revealed that he had been drunk yet again. The potential scandal had been effectively hushed up by his political friends in higher places. So, Frank's family name had remained unsullied, and he started his own farm implement store with the money he inherited. It quickly grew in sync with some outstanding crop years in Iowa. Because he thought he might have a future in politics, Frank made large donations to the red party like his father had done. Then a prolonged drought set in, and the economic collapse trashed his dreams.

Frank was not especially racist, but his paradigms aligned with other beliefs and conspiracy theories widely held by the red party's base. He ran for the House when his business finally went bankrupt because he really did not know what else to do. With lots of practice he became a confident and popular speaker who spoke plainly in a homespun manner. He told his Iowa audiences, convincingly, that he was suspicious of anything run by the government. He blamed the US government more than the Chinese government for the climate change that had financially ruined him, but he was adamant that both governments were at fault. He said, incorrectly, that the blue party was against personal freedom and the constitutional right of gun ownership. He successfully convinced people he was anti-scientists, anti-gays, anti-taxes, anti-abortions, anti-Muslims, anti-immigration, anti-vaccines, anti-masks, anti-social distancing and anti-woman's rights. And he won a long-held red district when the previous member had stepped down due to old age. And he did it by never saying what he was *for* politically.

Like his father, Frank had a drinking problem. Every other Friday night, he liked to play poker with some farmer friends, and then drive home drunk to his submissive wife and their suburban bungalow on the outskirts of Des Moines, Iowa. He always used quiet back roads. Unfortunately, he was somehow good at it, and he had never caused an accident, or been stopped by police and arrested.

***

Amos Merriweather was a lay preacher. He claimed he had studied divinity, but his claims were dubious. But no one challenged him because his guest-speaking engagements and 'sermons by invitation only' were so uplifting and inspiring. Rumours quickly circulated that he had performed miracles, and his following grew astronomically. He formed a charitable foundation called the Pure Christian Fellowship. He had briefly considered calling it the Pure White Christian Fellowship, but then guessed correctly that might be somewhat counterproductive. And then he started up a syndicated radio show called *Even A You Can Be A Saved*. He ended every show with a somewhat comedic, extremely popular, and almost melodic variation on the show's title: "Even a *yoooou* can be a *saaaaved*!"

The money was pouring in, and Amos figured he could shoot higher, and run for Congress. He was a natural speech maker who lied constantly without recourse to appease his followers. He was anti-abortion and so called pro-life, but completely oblivious to the suffering girls and women endured in some counties and even some states where abortions were once again illegal. He wore expensive jewellery, had five flashy luxury cars, owned two mansions and even a business jet. And he got away with advocating for personal poverty and charitable acts, while in the next breath asking for large donations to his Pure Christian Fellowship Foundation and his political campaigns. He alone knew that with creative accounting, a third of the funds that were directed to both causes were in truth going into his secret Cayman Island bank account. And he convincingly won his Congressional district in his southwestern state of New Mexico.

***

The four ultra-right-wing members of the House decided to form a political block to increase their political power and notoriety. And they decided they would use social media and stage protests to push their racist and populist, right-wing views. One of the populist ideas that they latched on to was that the Chinese government either was secretly behind the ZONT-2 project, or was secretly conspiring to take over the project and turn it into a space-based super weapon for destroying America.

Another populist idea that they actively promoted was that the greenhouse gas link to climate change was a hoax. In other words, they claimed climate change was a natural, recurring phenomenon that would just go away on its own. So, they said they believed there must be a conspiracy behind the hoax, probably led by green energy advocating oligarchs like Dufort and Semenov, who obviously, for selfish monetary advantage, just wanted to completely do away with the gasoline and diesel-powered vehicles that most Americans still loved to drive.

As their popularity grew, the money from the base started pouring in, and the American Gang of Four started to hold expensive and elaborate rallies with big-named country and western stars. And everyone who went to those rallies wore a red 'I'M A MERKAN' cowboy hat in honour of their locked-up hero Larry Rhodes. Everyone believed that Larry had been wrongly convicted, by conspirators of some sort, and Larry would someday, with Amos Merriweather's sacred blessing, and subsequent divine intervention, return to be the President of the United States of America.

The Gang of Four had a different and secret perspective. They hoped that when Larry got out of jail, he would become President of the white, wealth-craving and wealth-making part of America, or the only part that mattered to the gang, and to Larry.

35

Margaret Rushmore was a three-term US Senator. She was a staunch fiscal conservative, but she hated what her red party had devolved into during her lifetime, and where it seemed to be headed.

Margaret favoured a smaller federal government. To her that meant lower taxes, less regulation, wealthier free enterprises, more employment, and a growing economy. She favoured a strong military, with superior technology, but one designed to prevent wars or end them quickly, not win protracted wars started by US aggression, foolishness or greed. She thought everyone who could work, doing no matter what, *should* work and not have their hands out for social welfare. She thought people should look after their own family's heath care and education costs, and affordable private insurance should be available to help with that. After all, insurance companies generated wealth that could be taxed. In fact, to her all profit was good because it could be taxed, at a low rate, of course, to stimulate further investment. She wanted law and order but also the freedom to own a gun to defend herself, even though she had never in fact owned a gun. She knew gun ownership was a constitutional right, and she was quoted many times asking, 'who cares if other countries consider it a privilege and not a right?' She knew, but never mentioned, that those other countries had far lower gun death rates.

In her mind, Margaret thought protecting the constitution was the number one job of the President. In that respect alone, she stood out as different from the base of the red party, many of whom would support a one-party, fascist autocracy.

Margaret was also an isolationist who believed in tariffs to protect American jobs. She thought the UN was useless and a waste of money. She believed good infrastructure like roads, railways, airports, bridges, the internet and cell phone service could all be improved with private money and paid for by allowing tolls to be collected. Fundamentally, she believed people should pay for what they used.

But she also believed in science. So, she believed vaccines, masks and social distancing worked to end pandemics, and human activities like burning hydrocarbons and spreading fertilizer were undoubtedly causing climate change. She had rejected political donations from oil and gas lobby groups just on principles. She wanted to see a green economy, but one built with private, American money. She thought that American corporations were lagging their global green competitors because of populist disinterest and deliberate misinformation spread on social media and ultra-right-wing television networks by special interest groups and radical fringe groups, unfortunately like the American, and red party, Gang of Four.

Climate change was clearly a global problem, and Margaret started to wonder if she may have been wrong, and an improved and empowered UN might be a means to an end. China had been a threat to American financial and military security, but the situation in that far away and culturally different country had suddenly changed. The top-level coup raised her hopes for a thaw in the cold war, but these were early days yet. She distrusted Russia, and the EU too, because they pursued their own interests. But they did not seem especially aggressive or threatening these days.

And Margaret was at odds with many other members of the red party. She was not a racist. She believed in women's rights and the right of a woman to control her own body. She thought many so-called evangelicals were hypocrites, and that they said and did very un-Christian things. She thought homosexuality was an inherent human trait and should just be accepted as reality. She thought even subtly encouraging radical fringe groups to protest violently or threaten insurrection was destroying American democracy. The Gang of Four had recently crossed that line. And she considered the telling of truth as paramount and mandatory. She never lied and would hold other people accountable when they were clearly caught lying. She was famous on Senate committees for doing that, even with members of her own party, often when they were under oath.

And because she had become a political outlier, she was fearful about the upcoming mid-term election. Because of staggered timing, she was safe for a few more years, but her like-minded conservative friends in the US Senate that were up for re-election all felt extremely vulnerable with the rise of the radical Gang of Four. They expected there would be stiff challenges to their party nominations.

Polls were indicating that the House of Representatives would likely stay blue. There was a lot of popular support for the President and her blue administration. Most voters simply believed the folks in the White House were professional and doing a good job. The Senate was solidly red, but the radicalism of the Gang of Four could sway voters to move the Senate in the blue direction.

This was clearly a paradox. She was in the blue camp because she wanted the ZONT-2 facility to be built with US involvement, but only if US interests were protected, American jobs were created, it made economic sense, profits could be taxed, and global stability enhanced. And if the UN could ensure that no one country could turn the installation into a space weapon, well, that might make it totally agreeable.

But she also wanted the Senate to remain red. And if the Gang of Four all got to be Senators, not only would ZONT-2 not happen, but American democracy would also probably fail, and take the red party down with it.

36

On Sunday mornings, Senator Margaret Rushmore liked to walk with her black-haired Scottish terrier in Rock Creek Park in the District of Columbia. She had found that if she dressed like everyone else and wore a hat with her coat collars turned up, she was rarely recognized.

It was March 24, 2041. There was very little wind but there was a bit of a nip in the air. So, on this day Margaret had also wrapped a scarf around her neck. It also obscured the lower part of her face.

Before her Sunday walk, Margaret always stopped for a big paper cup full of dark roast coffee at a little booth at one entrance to the park. The cups came with a thick cardboard sleeve and were easy to hold onto without gloves. As she was adding some cream and sugar to her coffee, her little dog started to jump up on the leg of the woman standing beside her. The woman reached down to pet the dog, and said cheerfully, "Oh, you're a real sweety, aren't you!"

When the woman stood up again and looked back at her neighbour with the cute little dog, Margaret instantly assessed her as very pretty, sophisticated, cosmopolitan and possibly European. And then with a start, Margaret realized that she recognized the woman.

Margaret discreetly stepped away from the booth, with the dog's leash in her left hand and the cup of hot coffee in her right hand. The dog was obviously well trained and positioned itself behind Margaret's left heel. Margaret then motioned with a slight tilting of her head that the pretty lady should join her on her right side, or the coffee cup side. When they were walking side by side and well away from the booth, Margaret asked quietly, "You're Emma Baumgartner, aren't you?"

"Yes, and you're Senator Margaret Rushmore, aren't you? I must say, it is difficult to tell. That scarf is very effective if your desire is to remain anonymous."

"Yes, I'm Rushmore behind the scarf. This kind of anti-social behaviour is probably not going to help me get carved into *Mount*

Rushmore, but I'm too old to crave that sort of egotistical nonsense. And believe it or not, I'm rather an introvert.

"We have met before, madame, at a Senate Intelligence Committee hearing that I chaired. We asked for an expert to testify about industrial spying for us in a closed session. You did not have to do that, but we were glad you did."

"Yes, I remember. And I enjoyed that experience. It was also good for business. Rumours get out."

"Yes, they do. Washington is a sieve. So, what brings you to Washington, and this particular park at this particular time of day?"

"I love to go on long walks in parks, Senator Rushmore. And I think you suspect it was also with the hope that I could have a quiet, private chat with you."

"Okay. Thanks for being honest. Then you might as well call me Margaret. This is about as fast as I can go with my little dog, Toto. It's probably a comfortable, undistracting pace for both of us, too. So, what would you like to talk about, madame?"

"Please call me Emma, Margaret. I do some work for a wealthy industrialist. He's one of the key people behind the ZONT-2 project. I won't tell you his name, to protect all of us. He believes you want to see the project proceed, and he wants to help you break down some of the political barriers within the United States that are currently blocking it. But he does not want you to get into any trouble. Your help will be as discreet as it needs to be to maintain your comfort level."

"What exactly are we talking about help-wise?"

"We're not talking about political contributions, or kickbacks or anything illegal. We aim to embarrass your primary political opponents one at a time with scandalous revelations. I'm talking about the politicians who directly and maliciously threaten the ZONT-2 project. We were wondering if you would be interested in receiving advance warning of an upcoming revelation, say on a walk like this, with a different person each time to avoid arousing suspicion. Then you would be better prepared to take it the next step, politically."

"So, the people you represent have the power and the resources to do this covert *embarrassment* work?"

"Yes, and the intelligence and the guile and the experience."

"Really? What experience?"

"We ruined the political career of Larry Rhodes and helped put the filthy scum in jail."

The two women said nothing for a long while. It was a lovely day, and the natural sights and sounds in the scenic and wooded park were uplifting.

Finally, Margaret said, "Well, I hope to meet a few of your friends then on future walks like this. They probably should get themselves a cup of coffee like me, though, to make it look more natural. You know, just two chums casually walking along together, chatting about whatever. We'd better break it off now. You have a nice day, Emma."

"You too, Margaret. And your dog really is a sweety."

37

Exclusive Report
Freeworld Press
Atlanta, Georgia, USA
April 16, 2041

Freeworld Press has learned that a class-action lawsuit has been filed in a Georgia district court against Vicky Armstrong, a two-term member of the US House of Representatives. There are eighty-three plaintiffs listed in the suit which alleges hiring discrimination based on race, ethnicity or religion.

Armstrong owns a chain of twelve hair salons in the state of Georgia. In the past, she has defied all requests to appear before the House Ethics Committee to answer questions concerning possible conflicts of interest for allegedly failing to put control of her businesses fully in trust while she is a member of the House.

During her first term in office, Armstrong was also asked to appear before the House Judiciary Committee to answer charges of harassment against a novice, blue-party Representative, Juanita Hernandez, a woman of both Black and Hispanic heritage. When Armstrong refused to appear voluntarily, she was issued with a subpoena to appear before the Committee. The Committee heard from numerous witnesses that Armstrong had yelled racial slurs at Hernandez on numerous occasions in public, but never in the House. Also, video recordings show Armstrong pursuing Hernandez around the halls of Congress, attempting to taunt her into a public, even physical, confrontation. Despite the evidence, Armstrong refuted all the allegations before the Judiciary Committee. Acting upon the Committee's recommendation, the House administration fined Armstrong one-week's pay and told her to stop her abusive behavior.

Lawyers representing Armstrong and the plaintiffs in the civil suit that was just announced told Freeworld that no statements can be made to the press while the matter is before the court.

The Georgia Fair Employment Practices Act prohibits discrimination based on race, colour, disability, religion, sex, national origin or age. Georgia citizens are also protected under federal laws enforced by the EEOC or Equal Employment Opportunity Commission. Freeport has learned that the eighty-three plaintiffs have also filed a charge of discrimination against Vicky Armstrong with the EEOC.

Freeport talked to people outside two of the hair salons owned by Vicky Armstrong. Some people agreed to say a few words if they did not have to reveal their name. The comments were all digitally recorded. Here are a few excerpts:

"No, I've never seen a Black person in there. Worker or customer. Or anybody not lily white. That's why I come here. But don't quote me."

"Yes, I tried to get a job here. There was a 'hair cutter wanted' sign in the window saying to apply inside. I'm a qualified hair cutter with a five-year perfect work record. I quit for two years to raise my baby. I left my resume and references at the front counter, and never heard a freaking thing from them. As you can see, I'm Black. And no, I didn't know about a class-action lawsuit against Peachy Hair Salons, but I'm not surprised. I wonder why it took so long. Somebody must have worked incredibly hard to find those eighty-three people and help them file a suit together. I guess they missed me though, somehow. Maybe I'm not too late to get in there with them? I believe I'll check that out, though. Thanks for the info."

"I tried to get my hair done in there once. They told me they had no one qualified to cut coarse and curly African hair. In the state of Georgia? With all of us Black folks here? And they don't want that business? Come on! They just hate Black people, that's all."

"Everyone knows those folks in there are all racist. I don't have time for that garbage. I go somewhere else, where I'm treated like a human being."

"I have no tolerance for intolerance. I hope Vicky Armstrong gets fined into bankruptcy. And I hope she realizes she won't get another term in the House, let alone become a Senator. Georgia is bigger and better than her."

When asked to comment, the Majority Leader of the House, Susan McCarthy, declined, as she said the matter would eventually end up before the House Judiciary Committee. However, when asked to comment, the Majority Leader of the Senate, Margaret Rushmore, said, "The allegations against Representative Vicky Armstrong are truly disgusting. There is no place in America for people who use their position of business ownership, or political position, to engage in racist hatred and discrimination. And I assure you there is no place in the US Senate for such people either."

Vicky Armstrong recently announced her intention to run for the US Senate in Georgia in the upcoming mid-term election. Her campaign manager has refused to talk to Freeworld Press.

38

It was about seven-thirty in the morning on Saturday, May 4, 2041, and Frank Strange was loaded drunk. He had lost at poker heavily, and he suspected one of his so-called friends had cheated. The two middle-aged men had exchanged harsh words, and Frank had even taken a swing at the guy. The other four guys broke them apart and declared the game was over.

Everyone was drunk. It did not matter to the perennial farmer host that much, but his wife would be angry with him this time as the game had turned into an all-nighter. On poker nights, the four other regular, poker-playing guys took turns driving, as their farms were not that far away, and they figured they could co-pilot for the designated, but equally drunk, driver.

Frank lived farther away and so he was on his own. He had never asked for a lift, so he had never been offered one. With this bunch, after a hard night, there was no sober adult in the room to take his keys away from him. And the other guys did not pick up on the fact that Frank was staggering and slurring his speech. They just figured this was the same old Frank, the man who could hold his liquor and out drink anyone.

When Frank's car departed the lane to the farm and turned left to the east on a county road, a private detective posing as a private citizen called 911 to report a suspected drunk driver. The private detective had spent the night in a rusty old pick-up truck that was parked and backed into a field accessway about a hundred yards to the west of the lane to the farm. He also reported the car with the other four drunks after they drove by the front of his truck heading west, but he suspected they would probably all get home before they got caught.

Frank sped off down the gravel road towards Des Moines, Iowa. After a few blurry minutes, he realized he was speeding and struggling a bit to keep the car centered and between the steep side ditches. The roadbed was rounded and loosely gravelled in places. And this was an especially dangerous stretch of road, with culverts imbedded in accessways to farmers' fields. They basically formed vertical, rocky walls in the ditches. Fatalities were far too common, especially at night when drivers sometimes fell asleep at the wheel.

Frank forced himself to slow down and get into his imitation careful and sober driver routine. He had never seen a police car on this stretch of road and did not expect to see one at this early hour of the morning on a weekend.

Frank thought there might be something ahead of him on the road, but his reactions were horribly dulled, and he was now also a bit sleepy. Finally, he figured out there was police roadblock ahead. A car was just being let through a temporary wooden barrier after the driver had talked with two Iowa State Troopers.

In his confused state, Frank panicked. He was a selfish, self-centred man and his only thought was about himself. He said out loud, "This will ruin you, Franky boy!"

So, he hit the brakes as hard as he could. The four-door sedan weaved all over the road and narrowly avoided sliding into the left-hand ditch. When the vehicle had stopped, Frank backed up hard into the once trailing dust cloud. Then he realized he could not see the side ditches, so he stopped hard again. Then he figured he would do a three-point turn to reverse course and make good his escape. Seven uncoordinated points later, he was on his way again.

He was going about eighty miles an hour when he slowly slid into the righthand ditch. The car stayed upright somehow, but it had a crazy lean to the right. There was water in the ditch from an overnight thunderstorm, and thick black muck, and the car slowed quickly even though Frank still had the pedal to the metal. The car was going about twenty miles per hour when it hit a boulder-strewn field access way. The collision wrecked the front end of the car, and the airbag deployed.

Frank was a bit shaken up, but he was still heavily drunk and irrational. He decided his best course of action was to run away on foot into the right-side field. He struggled to free himself from his seat belt and the airbag, and then somehow climb out of the car. It was at a forty-five-degree angle, so the driver side door was incredibly heavy. But

Frank managed it with the help of an involuntary rush of panic-induced adrenaline, and he crawled his way free.

The accessway was gated, but Frank wormed his way between some rusty, galvanized steel, horizontal bars. Two small boys had been playing on the gate when the nearby collision with the accessway had occurred, but they were now standing together and shaking in fear about thirty feet back in the field.

Frank never saw the two boys. He fell awkwardly, but he struggled to his feet and started running into the field.

The Iowa State Police were not far behind him. A Trooper who had played as a defensive back for the Iowa State Cyclones football team easily hurdled the gate, ran him down, tackled him, and drove his face hard into the corn stubble. The two boys started clapping and laughing. Frank stopped resisting when the cuffs went on his wrists and he was dragged back to a police cruiser. He was taken to a State Police station on the outskirts of Des Moines. He blew two-and-a-half times over the legal blood alcohol limit. He was charged with driving while intoxicated, excessive speeding, recklessly endangering the lives of two children, resisting arrest, and leaving the scene of an accident.

During his trial, Frank's poker buddies confessed that Frank was undoubtedly drunk, and they should have done more to stop him from driving. They denied being drunk themselves, and they all had alibis for not being at home when the police came by for a visit after Frank's arrest. They basically had got into their tractors when they got home and driven far off into muddy fields. The judge heaped scorn and wrath on the five men, and publicly shamed them.

But then the judge turned her full, pent up anger on Frank. She suspended his licence for five years, fined him ten thousand dollars, and sentenced him to one year confinement in a medium security prison.

39

Exclusive Report
Freeworld Press
Washington, D.C.
June 8, 2041

Freeworld Press announced today that it has uncovered evidence that member Amos Merriweather of the US House of Representatives has secretly been diverting funds from his Pure Christian Fellowship Foundation, and his campaign financing organization, into a private Cayman Island bank account.

An undisclosed contact with the European Financial Intelligence Unit Network informed a Freeworld reporter that Merriweather's name had appeared in one of their investigations into an international money laundering scheme. Freeworld then tried to contact the small accounting firm that handles the financial books for both Merriweather's foundation and his campaign financing organization. Merriweather has recently shifted his political focus to a run for a US Senate nomination in New Mexico, and his fundraising is said to have been going very well. Freeworld left three messages over three days on the accounting firm's answering machine to explain what the call was about. On day four, the junior accountant with the firm called Freeworld, and claimed she had been advised by an undisclosed party that if she quote 'spilled the beans' she could plea bargain for leniency. She then emailed to Freeworld an image of a single page document that outlined how money had been flowing into Merriweather's Cayman Island bank account, and how taxes had been completely avoided.

Freeworld then notified the FBI and forwarded to them the electronic version of the single page document. The FBI has subsequently confirmed that it has involved the IRS and FinCen, or the Financial Crimes Enforcement Network, in a criminal investigation into the accounting firm's activities, and Amos Merriweather's involvement with skimming funds from two US-based funds, and then engaging in secretive and possibly illegal international money transfers.

In summary, Freeworld Press has discovered that Amos Merriweather is under investigation for theft, fraud, tax evasion and international money laundering. The House Judicial Committee just announced that it will be issuing a subpoena to Representative Merriweather to answer questions under oath before the Committee about his involvement in these highly suspicious if not illegal financial matters. Freeworld understands from undisclosed contacts that upwards of ten million US dollars could be involved.

40

Jim Garfield was dry fly fishing for rainbow trout in one of his favourite spots on the Elk River in West Virginia. The spot was below a stretch of the river known as 'The Dries' where the river re-emerges after flowing through three huge underground springs.

It was coming up to ten in the morning. It was a sunny day that was starting to get too hot for comfortable sport fishing in waterproof chest waders. Jim had started fishing at sunrise, and he was not having much luck. He could see fish rising in the smooth, slick-surfaced pools, but he just could not seem to match the hatch that was on the go with the selection of flies in his box. It was all catch and release anyway, and it was not like he needed a fish for his lunch.

He was about to start walking back down the left bank to his car that was parked on a gravel road about three miles away. But he heard the snap of a branch breaking upriver and was startled to see two burly younger men walking quickly downstream towards him on the left bank. They were wearing hiking boots, and clearly, they were not fisherman.

Jim quickly packed up his gear in a waterproof backpack and started walking downstream at a brisk pace. But then he saw two other burly young fellows walking quickly upstream towards him, also on the left bank.

Jim had no idea what this was about. He impulsively considered wading across the river, but it was too deep for him to manage safely with his chest waders and a wading stick. And then suddenly the four men were right beside him.

"Nice day... fellows," Jim stammered. "You guys out for a walk... a walk, or something?"

One of the men replied quietly, "Yes, we're here for something, all right. Something long overdue. We remember you, Jim Garfield. But it looks like you don't remember us. Have a closer look at the four of us."

Jim then studied the men's faces. And then he realized that he vaguely recognized two of the guys as players on one of the junior high school football teams that he had helped coach. The other two guys looked to be about the same age, with physiques that suggested they had once probably played football too.

Then a horrible part of Jim's earlier life flashed before his eyes. He panicked and dodged quickly away from the river, and the four men, to make a run for it downstream. But the men were far nimbler and unencumbered with chest waders and felt-lined wading boots. And they must have been expecting him to bolt. Two of the men grabbed him and dragged him over to a flat rock nearby. One of the men said, "Sit down, right there, Jim. That's good. Now, we're just going to have a little talk with you, that's all. There would be no sport in beating the hell out of you anyway, even though it might make us feel a bit better for a while."

"What do you guys want with… with me? I mean, after all of these years…"

"We want retribution for what you did to us when we were only fourteen years old, you perverted son of a bitch," growled one of the men.

Jim started to cry, mostly from fear, but also from the release of all the pent-up years of stress and angst as he had tried to pretend that he was not a paedophile. "So, you're going to… to kill me?" he wailed in anguish.

"No, Jim, we're not murderers, but we *are* going to offer you a choice," said the man doing most of the talking. Jim was frustrated that he could not remember anyone's name. And that confirmed his interest in them had not been as students and developing young football players, but rather as exploitable, sexual objects.

"You see, a private detective tracked us all down, and got us talking to each other," the man continued. "We realized that we were not alone. You molested all of us. And suddenly we have strength in numbers. And apparently someone with a lot of money is willing to take you down in civil court by paying for the best lawyers in Virginia. The lawyer we talked to said he'll burn you for all you've got. It seems he knows Coach Butler is willing to testify that he knows you went after quarterback Billy Cramer, that is, you tried to rape him. Coach thought there might have been others, but no one else came forward. That was our mistake. And his mistake was to encourage you to quit your teaching job rather than to call the cops on you, then and there. He said he'll admit to all that under oath.

"You see, Jim, Coach Butler wants to clear his conscience and finally move on. And so do we. So, here are your two choices. You'll let us take you to a mental hospital nearby, where you have an appointment at four this afternoon with a psychiatrist. If you spill your soul, and he checks you in to the institution for further evaluation and treatment, we'll let the system take care of you.

"Or you can stay in a fantasy world of denial. And we will all help to completely ruin you in court. That means no more member of the House of Representatives, and no more dreams of being a US Senator."

Jim was still whimpering and crying a bit. Then he suddenly got angry and snapped, "You guys would ruin yourselves too! So, I don't believe what you say!"

"No, Jim," the spokesman replied quietly. "We're way beyond that now. If it all comes out in court, that will just be the start of a long overdue healing process for us. You see, we all talked to the same psychiatrist you'll be meeting soon. That is, if you want to. It's all up to you."

"There's a third choice, you bastards!" Jim yelled. "There's a gun in my car, and I'll blow my freaking brains out!"

"No, Jim, we won't let you do that," the young man continued calmly. "If you make a move to do that, we'll all sit on you while we call 911 for some help from the State Police."

Then Jim seemed to fade away into a zone where he could internalize all the stages of dealing with trauma. The four young men waited patiently, while watching Jim's face intently. The ensuing ten minutes felt like four hours. When Jim seemed to have reached some form of temporary inner peace, the spokesman asked quietly, "What's it going to be then, eh? Tell us, Jim."

Jim sighed, shook his head, and said with a wavering smile, "I guess we should go see your psychiatrist friend, boys."

They helped him to his feet without saying any more to him. Then they walked downstream along the left bank in single file, with two of the men in front of Jim, and the other two men behind him.

41

Senator Margaret Rushmore was startled to see that this time it was Emma Baumgartner in the flesh standing right next to her, stirring cream into her cup of coffee. They were both at the solitary little booth outside a gate to Rock Creek Park in Washington D.C. But Margaret smoothly disguised her initial internal reaction. She casually backed away from the booth with her little dog's leash in her left hand and her cup of steaming, dark roast coffee in the other. Then she slightly tilted her head to suggest Emma should walk beside her on her right side.

The plain clothed security man nearby saw the head tilt too and he nonchalantly started walking behind the two ladies at more than his usual safe distance. The subtle, but deliberate head movement, suggested his boss was cool with the whole thing.

It was early in the morning on Sunday, August 25, 2041, and it was looking to be a muggy, partly cloudy day. Thunderstorms were predicted later that afternoon. The two ladies were wearing light summer dresses. Their attire was entirely practical, but it meant that they could be easily recognized by others enjoying the park.

After they had walked a few hundred paces, Margaret said quietly, "I was surprised to see that it was you today, Emma. Frankly, I did not expect to ever see you again."

"Yes, I guess there is a simple message in my actual presence here today. The man I work for is wondering if we are now at a nexus, and if there was something more that he could be doing from your perspective to help move ZONT-2 along."

"No there isn't, and I think he, and presumably you, have done quite enough. The American Gang of Four is now the Gang of Zero. It was all done very neatly, with a great deal of discretion, and even a touch of elegance and compassion."

"That's always a preferred methodology to avoid suspicion. They all presented us with ready made avenues to bring them down. There was no need to invent anything or even consider breaking the law."

"Yes. The gang members were all ardent supporters of Larry Rhodes, and they had banked heavily on him becoming President. The reasons for their fanaticism are now all too evident. Rhodes was completely corrupt, and the members of the gang thought he would and could grant them immunity from prosecution. So, they all figured if they could keep getting re-elected to the House, or better yet, move up the ladder to the Senate, then they could continue with their evil ways. But then the metaphoric hammer of fate nailed them to crosses of their own making."

"So, has your political situation changed at all?"

"Yes, considerably. The fringe right in the red party has suffered a real blow and may be neutered for a while. But it won't last long, unfortunately. They have been the dominant force in our party for twenty-five years or so. But right now, they are in disarray, and I have managed to re-form a block of moderate conservatives, probably fifteen out of the fifty-four sitting red-party US Senators. There is a similar block re-forming in the House I understand, but that is not my doing."

"So, will this factor into next year's November midterms?"

"Yes, possibly. The House should stay blue, unfortunately. Voters are probably glad to see the 'Gang of Loudmouths' gone. Polls suggest that anyway. Even if we put moderate conservatives up for election in their places, the sentiment is leaning towards the blue side.

"The US Senate is different. Nationwide popular opinion does not matter as much when it comes to the Senate. States with very little population like red South Dakota have the same two US Senate seats as blue California, which has the same population as all of Canada. So, I believe we can retain a slim majority."

"So, does that mean even after the mid-term elections, there will not be enough support to pass the bill that enables ZONT-2 to proceed?"

Margaret said nothing for a long while. She smiled back at a few people passing by who clearly had recognized her. Then she said quietly, "Not necessarily. No, and the bill is something I intend to fight hard for. I've done my research, and I'm convinced ZONT-2 is in America's best interest. I will tell my fellow conservative-block-members that since the fringe right were against it, we need to be *for* it, and strongly so. But there are lots of other reasons to be *for* it, and I'll probably annoy and or bore the heck out of my cohorts and the media by incessantly talking about those things."

"So, there's a chance the bill that passed in the House earlier this year might have a chance to pass in the US Senate before the midterm results next November?"

"Possibly. We'll see. A lot of things must go right. And if they do, I suspect you know the President has already said she would sign the bill immediately."

"Okay. Then I can pass on to you my client's view that time is of the essence, now more than ever, and not just in America. As you know, China is currently, or at least outwardly, stable and rational, but it is uncertain how long that will last. A commercial deal is basically done with them, although the US and possibly the most powerful EU nations might need to sway them to lessen their demands for a Communist-leaning, or China-favouring, board of directors. With China included, there are thirty-six countries willing to put up capital in exchange for a proportional share of the revenue, or actual power in the form of beamed energy. The US would make thirty-seven participating countries in total."

"We're not talking about equal shares of the capital and revenue streams, are we?"

"No, if the US helps make this project happen, we see three tiers of contributors for Stage One. The US, the EU nations as an aggregate group, and China would be in Tier One. The UK, Russia, Canada, India, Brazil, Japan, South Korea, Saudi Arabia, South Africa and Australia would be in Tier Two. The rest would fit into Tier 3. The investment money in each tier would be the same. Also, the split would be the same for all countries in each tier. This means the EU would be treated as if it were a sovereign country inside the deal. And to appease the UN, no one country can ever be allowed to own more that ten percent of the corporation after any stage of development. This will be clearly stipulated in a new space law we hope the UN will pass after our commercial deals with participating countries are fully executed."

"I see. With the application of a bit of algebra, that will help my staff put a useful scalar on our piece of the pie. And if we come along, will the EU nations follow?"

"We think so, but the US might need to twist a few European arms a bit."

"Well, we've done that before. We didn't twist an arm right off, so it might work again. Anything else on your mind today?"

"No, that's about it."

"Well, you've given me lot to think about, but that's a good thing. Have a nice day, Emma."

"You too, Margaret. And you too, Toto! What a sweety you are!"

42

It was three o'clock in the afternoon on November 11, 2041. No words were spoken in the cavernous and historic Oval Office as the newspaper press reporters were allowed to take some pictures, and the major network television cameras were allowed to capture a live feed. The four VIPs who were sitting comfortably in the formal living room part of the Oval Office were all smiling, but the smiles looked a bit forced.

After what seemed like enough time, President Kate Winslow said cheerfully, "Thanks, everyone. I'll just make a brief statement before we ask you all to leave so we can begin a private discussion with our honoured guest, Senate Majority Leader Margaret Rushmore.

"As you can see, joining me today for this discussion will be Vice President Christos Balaskas, and White House Chief of Staff Harold Penobscot. Among other things, we expect to talk about the two bills that are currently before the US Senate for approval, and what might be required to get them passed. In other words, we hope to explore the common ground with our esteemed colleague and American patriot, Senator Rushmore, and the key points of contention, of course. I believe, wholeheartedly, that America can only benefit from frank, respectful and open discussions like these. Now, if you can all make your way out of the Oval Office, that would be great."

One reporter called out, "If it's an open discussion, why can't we stay?"

Another reporter yelled, "This is all about ZONT-2, isn't it?"

Press Secretary Mary Walker then stepped forward, with the television cameras still operating, and said loudly, "Now, you all heard what the President said. That's all the time we can spare for you today. There could be a few statements in the Rose Garden after their meeting, and if so, there may also be some time to take a few questions from the press gallery. Now, come on, pack it up, folks, and move it along. That's great, keep it moving, that's it. Here, sir, you dropped this. Looks expensive, but I don't think it's broken. Okay, that's good. The last of the stragglers now, great, great..." And then over her shoulder, Mary loudly called out cheerfully, "I hope you enjoy your visit, Senator Rushmore! And I'll now close this big old door for you folks."

When the main office door was closed, President Kate Winslow was the first to speak. "Thank you for coming to chat with us, Margaret. It looks like a hallway conversation between two junior staff members may have kicked this off. Regardless, it's been a long time since red and blue thought a closed-door, face-to-face discussion might be value adding. America had been so completely partisan for decades."

"Yes, and I am not here to suggest that a new era of so-called bipartisanship is beginning," Margaret replied bluntly. "There have been few instances in American history where anything approaching cooperation on most matters has occurred. Although perhaps some degree of it occurred during a world war when things looked especially grim for our mutual survival."

"Yes, I think you're right, Margaret. But would not climate change be an equivalent crisis to a world war?"

"Yes, I believe so. But there are still many people in the red party who deny climate change, and who harbour something approaching real, foaming-at-the-mouth hatred for anything blue. And I know there are people so far to the left in the blue party that they would even be viewed as die-hard communists up there in left-leaning Canada."

"Okay, so has something changed recently, that might allow us to explore commonality?"

"Perhaps. The demise of the so-called Gang of Four has temporarily stunned and silenced the extreme right wingers. A few staunch moderate conservatives, like myself, are of a mind that we may be able to win a few battles in the public forum for a short while."

"Could one of those battles be to see the ZONT-2 bill passed?"

"Possibly. I may be able to sway enough Senators to vote with me in support of it, with a few amendments. But they will need to be able to hold something up to both the moderate conservatives and the extreme right-wing base that will be viewed as concessions from the blue party."

"Well, that's about as frank as it gets. So, we will need to provide for some face-saving measures to get anything done?"

"Yes. Some horse-trading, followed by both sides claiming victory in the media scrums."

"Yes. I believe that may have once been referred to as the old Potomac Two-Step."

Margaret laughed, and said, "Yes, I think that may be right. So, do you want to dance, Kate, or sit this one out?"

"I would prefer to dance with my husband, but since no one else is looking, or listening, why not?"

"Okay. Then let me lay out the field of battle, or rather the grounds for a negotiation. So, let's see, you want the House's bill in support of ZONT-2 to pass through the Senate. So do I, but that's a moot point as I'm only one of a hundred US Senators. The forty-six blue Senators are presumably all in favour of it, is that right? Nods around the room, so we'll take that as a given. So, we need at least three more red Senators to come to the dance with us assuming the Vice President will cast the deciding vote to settle a tie."

"And I will certainly cast that vote to pass this world-saving bill," interjected Christos Balaskas with unrestrained passion.

"Thanks, Chris. We knew we could count on you. Now, you mentioned a couple of amendments though, Margaret?"

"Yes, firstly, we will need to see stronger wording about what is acceptable to the US with respect to the twelve countries that will nominate representatives to the joint venture corporation's board of directors. To partially appease China, we could live with Vietnam replacing Canada. The Canadians are our number one trading partner and our closest ally. They will undoubtedly let us represent them, and the North and Central American region. Mexico will probably support the resolution in the UN as they are part of the trade agreement that includes Canada and the UK. But we might only get half of the Central American countries to vote in favour of the UN resolution. There is some bad blood between us that we might struggle to resolve with say, trade concessions, or the relaxation of some immigration laws.

"Secondly, we see no issue at all with replacing Argentina with the Congo.

"And thirdly, and lastly, there is no way we can accept Cuba replacing South Africa, and Kuwait replacing Saudi Arabia."

"That's mostly along the lines of what we were discussing just yesterday, Madam President," offered Chief of Staff Harold Penobscot.

"Yes, I agree, Harold. So, we can probably accommodate that, Margaret. What's the second amendment you're looking for in the ZONT-2 bill?"

"We like proposing Los Alamos as the site of the first US-based power receiving station. The political optics are magnificent."

"Yes, and I note the site is conveniently in New Mexico, currently a red state."

"Yes. And we want to see west Texas named as the second site, and central Alaska as the third site."

"And I note again that those are also currently red states. A couple of things occur to me, though. We only need to name one site in the bill as it only applies to Stage One. When Stage One is completed, the total power beamed to the Earth will only be about seven-hundred and fifty megawatts, and it makes sense to split that power three ways. Putting another receiving station in northern Australia, and another in central Saudi Arabia, effectively blankets the world, and allows fewer relay satellites to be required, since the Earth rotates and the power will be delivered twenty-four hours per day, year-round.

"But we could agree to draft a new and separate bill that names, and orders by priority, the location of power receiving sites in America for the future stages of the project. Would that be agreeable?"

"Possibly. You just raised some good points. Okay, let's park that as agreeable for now."

"Great. Now, is there something else we need to focus on with our horse-trading today, or rather, our *negotiation*?"

"Yes, one other thing. It's the other bill that the blue House sent to the red Senate. I'm referring to the three-point-five *trillion* dollar, so called infrastructure bill. It's really a poorly disguised, *pork barrel* bill, and we want to see it reduced by one trillion dollars."

Kate Winslow quickly exchanged meaningful glances with Christos and Harold. She could tell they were also reading this the same way. Kate's excitement and elation just went through the roof, and the other two men were obviously struggling to stay outwardly passive.

The infrastructure bill laid out a spending plan or policy for the next ten years. And all that spending could be overridden by future bills, when the House and Senate demographics might be different, and or overridden by the standard budgetary approval bills. In the greater scheme of things, considering the peril the nation and the world are facing, agreeing to concessions, and trimming that infrastructure bill, would pale in significance. This meant that Rushmore wanted to do a deal! She really *did* want to see ZONT-2 proceed!

Without missing a beat, Kate replied smoothly with, "Very well, Margaret. Let's hear what fat you'd like to remove from the so-called pork barrel bill..."

43

Farkas Timko was the Prime Minister of Hungary. In theory, Hungary was still a parliamentary constitutional republic within the European Union and NATO. However, Hungary had devolved over the last three decades into a rogue autocracy, and a continual thorn in the side of both the EU and NATO.

Hungary was notorious for always voting against legislation in the European Parliament, hoping for, and sometimes getting, more favourable terms in revised legislation. And it was completely at odds with the rest of Europe with respect to accepting refugees, especially non-white refugees. It had erected walls and fences around its border and made it difficult for even some EU passport holders to visit the country for business or pleasure.

Farkas and his predecessor had used back-to-back global pandemics first to grab on to dictatorial power within Hungary, and then to consolidate it. The Hungarian National Assembly, or parliament, and its right-wing majority had granted the Prime Minister emergency powers. It was left entirely up to the Prime Minister to decide when the crises were over, and when it would be safe to hold another election.

Using hurried legislation and bully tactics, one of the first things Farkas did as Prime Minister was to get rid of the President position. The President used to perform an oversight role, and a change-of-parliament stewardship role. But Farkas argued that the role had become mostly ceremonial, and sometimes obstructive to getting things done efficiently.

The people of Hungary had now given up waiting for a return to democracy. Farkas could rule by decree for an indefinite period with no effective oversight. And the EU had proven to be a paper tiger, and powerless to stop Hungary's move towards a form of racist fascism.

Farkas was now fifty-eight years old. He had been married to the same woman for thirty-four years. She willingly played the part of the

Prime Minister's wife when that was necessary, but the love spark between them had vanished long ago.

Farkas was still a distinguished-looking and ruggedly handsome man. He was always well-groomed, with just a touch of grey in his sideburns and in his short brown hair. Women still found him attractive, and he still had sexual urges. But Timko decided he would never risk the scandal of being found with a prostitute. He was proud of the fact that his first name meant 'wolf' in Hungarian, and he unabashedly considered himself a bit of a sexual predator. So, he waited patiently until safe and discreet opportunities for 'natural' fornication arose, and then he was quick to pounce.

Farkas had used public money to build a five-star restaurant exclusively for the use of top Hungarian government officials with their large, publicly funded, expense accounts. It was adjacent to the National Assembly Building in Budapest. The restaurant manager knew the Prime Minister liked to see young, pretty and voluptuous waitresses and chef assistants in the restaurant. And he knew that 'Farkas the Wolf' always looked forward to seeing new prey. So, the female staff turnover in the restaurant was high by design.

One day during lunch, Farkas was struck by the ravishing, innocent and youthful beauty of a new server. The girl had long blonde hair, and an hourglass figure that her poorly fitting waitress uniform could not disguise. She seemed quite willing to chit-chat with him, and even flirt a bit. She said her name was Candace, and that she had taken the job in the inner government restaurant after failing her first year of college. She admitted to being a poor student.

After lunch, when Candace brought the check for Farkas to initial, he mentioned in a cavalier manner that if Candace ever got bored with her server job, perhaps she might consider being a maid. He said he only brought the subject up because a maid had just quit in his second villa in Budapest where his wife liked to spend a lot of her time. Candace said she would indeed be interested in such a job. So, Farkas suggested she might like to visit the villa, and get to meet his wife, after her restaurant shift finished at five p.m. Candace seemed impressed that Farkas, the busy Prime Minister, knew when her shift would end. She agreed to his suggestion, and Farkas said he would arrive with his chauffeured limousine to pick her up at the front door of the restaurant precisely at five p.m.

Candace emerged from the restaurant wearing a long woolen winter coat. It was early December, and a windy, cold day in Budapest.

When they entered the villa together, they took off their coats and Farkas hung them up in an entranceway closet. Farkas was instantly turned on when he saw that Candace was wearing a very tight pair of designer blue jeans and a tight, thin, satiny top that revealed her flat stomach and midriff. She was not wearing a bra. Farkas somehow managed to hide his now raging lust, and calmly called out for his wife. When there was no response, he pretended to consult his smartphone, and told Candace that he was sorry, it looked like he had missed a note from his wife that morning. It seemed that her sister was feeling poorly, and she was spending a few days with her in a country estate in the north of Hungary. Farkas apologised for not being able to explain the maid position as well as his wife could have managed. But he offered to show Candace around the place himself. Candace agreed to the offer with an excited smile.

For some reason, Farkas first led Candace to what he called his 'Wolf's Den'. It was a combination study, museum and library. Candace stayed very close to him at all times. There was a large table in the room filled with model missiles and rockets. Farkas explained he made them all when he was a boy, and they had sentimental value. Candace told him the workmanship was remarkable.

She did not tell him that she knew many of the missiles were modern and were not around when Farkas had been a boy.

There were framed photographs of Hungary's nuclear power plants on the walls of the den, and even a scale model of one of Hungary's newest nuclear facilities. At least half of Hungary's electricity was generated by Russian-designed, pressurized water, natural or slightly enriched uranium, nuclear reactors. In the Soviet era, Hungary sourced the uranium it needed from the USSR, and sent the spent radioactive fuel back to Russia. Farkas explained this all to Candace as she moved another step closer to him, and he proudly added that under his leadership, Hungary was now mining its own uranium, buying it from all over the world, and performing its own enrichment.

Candace silently noted that Farkas did not say Hungary was secretly building breeder reactors, secretly extracting plutonium from spent nuclear fuel, and enriching some uranium to weapons-grade, or ninety percent U-235, or the most fissile isotope component in natural uranium. He also did not reveal that he was about to pull Hungary out of the global, nuclear non-proliferation treaty.

Candace then noticed a large, framed map on a wall in the den. She moved so close that their bodies were in physical contact, and she asked what the map represented. Farkas explained that it showed the origin of the Hungarian people. When she seemed to be as intensely interested in the map as she was in him, he explained that the Finnish and Hungarian people were members of the Finno-Ugric branch of the Uralic languages, and that a dozen or so languages were still spoken in countries bordering the Urals. He specifically mentioned the Khanty and Mansi people who lived in modern-day Russia, or Western Siberia.

Candace was nodding with eyes-wide-open awe at his vast knowledge. So, with his ego appropriately stroked, Farkas added that Estonian and Lappish also belong to this language group. He said scholars disagreed on dates, but perhaps in four thousand BC or so a group of hunters from the Siberian lands beyond the Urals split apart, and the Finnish group migrated towards the Baltic, and the Ugric group moved southward and westward towards present-day Hungary. He said they became proficient nomadic herdsmen through contact with Turkic peoples. And the presence of many Turkish words in modern Hungarian showed that Finno-Ugric could be linked with other languages of central Asia.

Farkas said nothing about the bold, red, hand-drawn line on the map that enclosed the region around the countries of Hungary, Ukraine, Belarus, the Baltic countries, Finland and a great swathe of Russia that included the Khanty-Mansiysk Okrug. Candace pretended not to notice the red line. Instead, she just smiled seductively, and asked when he was going to show her the master bedroom.

Farkas grabbed her by the hand and let her quickly to the bedroom. Their clothes were off in a flash. And then their lovemaking was wildly athletic, and Candace was insatiable. Finally, Farkas just had to cry out, "Enough!" and they rolled apart. He lit a cigarette while Candace stroked the thick mat of greying brown hairs on his chest. He stared at the ceiling and seemed lost in thought.

Candace asked sweetly what he was thinking about. He lied at first, and said he was only thinking about her, and how exciting she was compared to other women he had slept with. Then she asked if he was also thinking about the interesting map on the wall of his den, or his beautiful model missiles, or the country's proud nuclear power heritage. He then admitted that he was indeed thinking about all those things, and about what they meant, and how they were all part of his dream for what he then called 'a greater Hungary'. She asked him to tell her about his dream, and she promised to listen very closely, even if he decided to use big words again that she would not be able to understand.

Farkas Timko had never told anyone his dream or committed anything to writing. And it had been a long time since he had revisited it himself. His inner cabinet members suspected elements of it but had never been able to piece it all together.

But because of his exceptional masculine charm and virility, here was this submissive and inert 'sounding board' in the pleasant form of an innocent young bimbo laying down beside him. So, he felt safe with re-working his plan and his dream out loud.

He started with a lecture about how Hungary had once blossomed when it had formed a union with Austria. He said the union was busted up by World War One, but it would never have lasted anyway. He explained that Austria was to the west, and it was far more natural for Hungary to look to the east, where its ethnic roots lay. And Hungary had yet to recover from World War Two, and the years wasted under the malicious, imperialistic, and exploitive fist of the Soviet Union. He said that was a period analogous to the Mongol invasion and rule of Russia, which had kept that country from sharing in the European Renaissance.

Then Farkas explained, more to himself than to Candace, how he alone could build Hungary into a global power. He said it just needed a few nuclear weapons and intercontinental ballistic missiles to start it off. He would pick off countries to the east using subversion, terror tactics and blackmail, as Hitler had done during the build-up to World War Two, after starting with his native Austria. The EU and NATO were powerless to stop him, and so was the UN. They were all completely dysfunctional and cowardly. And even though not all the countries on his hit list were ethnically Finno-Ugric-Hungarian, just like Hitler had realized for his Third Reich, Hungary needed 'living space' to allow the pure racial strain to grow so it could dominate the rest of the world. The impure races would simply be displaced to other countries or liquidated.

He suddenly noted that Candace had been quiet for a long while. Then he saw that the disrespectful, impudent little wench had seemingly fallen asleep on him! And while he was literally baring his soul, too! That greatly angered him, so he shook her awake and told her to put her clothes back on. Then he packed her up in his limousine and told his driver to take her back to the parliament restaurant. He told her cruelly that she could make her own way home from there. She seemed terribly hurt by his cold-heartedness, but he blew her tears off completely.

The next day Candace was fired when she dropped a bowl of goulash on the floor of the kitchen, splashing the pantleg of the head chef in the process.

And five days later, Candace met up with Emma Baumgartner for a walk in a Budapest city park. She told Emma all about what had happened, and all that she had heard from Farkas Timko, even while she had pretended to be asleep. She also expanded upon what she had found out about Hungary's secret nuclear program during a separate evening soiree with another older man who was equally unhappy with his marriage.

Then Emma slipped Candace a thick envelope filled with large-denomination euro notes and thanked her for a job well done. And then they talked about how Candace was coming along with her master's thesis in theoretical nuclear physics at the University of Bucharest in Romania.

44

Alain Dufort shook hands with Timofey Semenov and Holt Carson when they arrived at the two-room business centre suite. Alain had long-term leased the suite from the Hotel des Bergues in Geneva, Switzerland. The suite was swept every day by espionage experts, who looked for illicit listening devices. They had never found any, but Alain suspected just the knowledge that daily sweeps were made had kept is enemies at bay.

It was the first time in over a year that the three men had met in person.

Alain had a palatial office in the Wardenclyffe Corporation's forty-eight storey tower in Geneva. But he found the rented business centre and the other amenities that the classy, fully equipped and ultra-secure hotel offered made for a more pleasant and productive experience when he was meeting with distinguished visitors. His guests usually took up his suggestion to book themselves a luxurious room in the hotel, which made everything very convenient.

It was December 20, 2041, and the nurturing and calming feel of Christmas was in the air. It was six o'clock in the morning, and most of the evening Christmas lights were still aglow in the very still and otherwise dark city.

The men were all early risers. They quickly got settled with their laptops open in front of them around a large, circular table in the main room in the suite. The other room could be closed off by a door so private, secure, cellphone calls could be made. The main room also had a kitchen area, a bar, a couple of comfortable leather-covered coaches and chairs, and a few end tables and lamps.

After exchanging a few pleasantries about yesterday's long and uneventful journeys by business jets, and the traditional Christmas atmosphere in Geneva, the three men got down to work.

Timofey, Holt and their carefully selected executives had been working to put in place separate Memorandums of Understanding with countries notionally interested in financially participating in the ZONT-2 project. And Alain and his executives and top-notch hired consultants had focused on advancing the requisite UN resolution, or new space law, while at the same time lobbying for support from UN General Assembly nations.

All their work was iterative, with as many frustrating reversals as advances. So, frequent videoconference check-in meetings had been required over the previous year.

"So, Holt, why don't you start us off today?" Alain began. He had been picking up and enjoying some of Holt's Texas slang, so he then asked, "Where the heck are we, anyway, Tonto? I've lost the gosh darn trail again."

Holt laughed, and then he replied while scratching his chin, "Well, Kemosabe, I reckon we're close to seeing a finish line, or at least we're closer than we've ever been before. We now have MOUs with the US and China. And all the Tier One, Tier Two and Tier Three countries are mapped out in the over-arching charter document, as well as the cost sharing splits, and the power and or revenue sharing splits. The remaining stumbling block is the EU.

"I met with the President of the European Commission yesterday in Brussels. You probably know her name is Geerten De Vries, and she's Dutch. It was an awkward meeting for the both of us. She must have said the word 'unanimity' to me ten times! It seems our agreement with the EU must be considered the same as a comprehensive trade agreement. Therefore, one-hundred percent unanimity will be required to consummate our deal.

"I get the sense that she might not like Americans very much, or at least ones with Texas accents. It might be best if you met with her next time, Timofey…"

"She might not like Russian *cheloveks* either, Holt, but we can work it that way, I'm sure," Timofey interjected.

"Okay, great, thanks Tim," Holt continued. "Anyway, it seems all the EU nations are just about on board, with unanimity, except for Hungary.

"Yumping yiminy crickets, I *hate* that unanimity word! But I digress, sorry.

"De Vries told me Hungary has presented the EU with a long list of demands that are not in any way related to our project. I'm talking about stuff like tougher immigration laws, new intra-EU tariffs, cancellation or major revisions of international trade agreements, a relaxation of pollution and labour laws, a far tougher stance against Russia, and a weakening of NATO's power and strength. She confided that Hungary's demands are irrational in totality, and seemingly at cross purposes. But there is one thing that might have a direct bearing on us. Hungary apparently wants to become a dominant, or *the* dominant, European rocket launcher."

"Yes, I can vouch for that," Alain interjected. "The Hungarian Prime Minister, Farkas Timko, has sent me a letter, saying he wants my EU rocket manufacturing and launching company to completely migrate to Hungary. He also says he wants it to start making intercontinental ballistic missiles, to quote, 'sweeten my pie and put Hungary firmly on the map'. He didn't out right offer me a very large kickback bribe, but he came awfully close to doing that.

"My EU rocket company has manufacturing facilities in seven European countries. That makes economic sense with the vast, hi-tech and complicated supporting supply chain properly considered, and the favourably transparent borders within the EU with respect to tariffs and labour laws.

"But I want to first share with you today some startling and disturbing intelligence I have recently received from Emma Baumgartner. It's about what this Farkas Timko guy is really up to."

Alain reached into his briefcase, pulled out two folders and then handed one each to Timofey and Holt. The folders each contained the same five-page document. Then he said, "I'll make a phone call in the next room, while you guys read that document. No one else but me has read it. Believe me, you guys won't be telling me later that it was a waste of your time to take a close look at it."

When Alain returned to the main room in the suite about fifteen minutes later, Holt and Timofey were both silently and angrily scratching notes on their copies of the document. Alain sat down and waited while intently watching the other men's faces. It was obvious they were both upset by what they had read.

Timofey was the first to say something. "How reliable is this information, Alain?" he growled. "I mean, the implications are completely staggering if it's all true."

"It is as sure as anything and everything that comes from Emma Baumgartner," Alain replied calmy. "Her stuff has always been one-hundred percent spot on during my long business relationship with her."

"The guy is a Hitler wannabee!" Holt blurted out in anger. "He wants to conquer the world after he steals all of Eastern Europe and a big chunk of Russia!"

"I will most definitely have to share this verbatim with the GRU, Alain, and Holt," Timofey immediately added slowly and carefully. He was clearly trying to control his pent-up emotions. "It potentially reveals a direct threat to Russia. Russia paid a higher price than any nation in World War Two. There will never be another deal made with a devil to delay a conflict, like what Stalin did to split half of a quickly conquered Poland with Hitler. We know appeasement is not an option. Tyrants just want more and more and lie to your face.

"And you just *can't* let him have your EU rocket company, Alain."

"No, you are right about that, Tim," Alain replied through clenched teeth. "Don't worry, that's not even something I would consider. But I thought you would say what you did about going directly to the GRU with this document, and I think that's the best move you can make for all of us. And, Holt, I'll now share the document with my Swiss FIS contact, and suggest that he in turn shares it with *all* the allied intelligence agencies, including the CIA."

"Okay, thanks," Holt replied. He looked more puzzled now than angry. "So, this development is much bigger than the three of us can handle, and our organizations can handle, as big as they are. It may be best to wait and see how the world reacts to this, when it gets out somehow, or at least what transpires next within the EU, and NATO. And I think we need to make sure the press does not get a hold of this, or at least not yet. But what do you guys think?"

"I agree, we charge on with everything else as if we did not see this damning document from Emma," Alain replied confidently while looking intently at Timofey's now inscrutable face.

After an awkwardly long silence, Timofey said icily, "I predict we will not have to wait long for something to happen that will help our cause, and Russia's cause. Oh, there will be a slight delay while facts are checked and confirmed. And another slight delay while the wheels are put in place. But then the Trans-Siberian Express will start rolling, and when that happens, it is unstoppable."

After another awkward moment, Holt abruptly stood up and said, "Okay, guys, it's early for a break. But I think I'll put a pot of coffee on for us. It might not completely cool off our tempers, but it might allow each of us to catch our breath so we can move on with our meeting."

"Right, Holt!" Alain replied cheerily. "Good idea. The coffee pouches are in the cupboard to the left of the sink."

After a few moments, Timofey seemed to relax a bit, and he said quietly with a bit of a smile, "Yes, guys, a cup of coffee sounds good."

45

NEWS FLASH:

Budapest, Hungary, January 12, 2042, 18:31 GMT: Freeworld Press is reporting that Farkas Timko, the Prime Minister of Hungary, and an unidentified female companion, have been found dead in a villa in Budapest. The cause of death is unknown but physical signs apparently point to death by asphyxiation, although a police official told a Freeworld Press reporter off the record that there were no signs of strangulation on either body. Forensic analyses are underway, and an autopsy will be performed on both corpses.

Budapest City Police have notified Timko's wife of thirty-four years, Edlyn Zambo, of her husband's death. She immediately made it known to police that she will not be talking to newspaper, television or any other media reporters.

The Hungarian National Assembly, or parliament, is now in an extended emergency session. It is expected that the members of the Assembly will pass legislation to restore former President Deco Fekete to the office he once held. Fekete would then be able to lead the country during an interim period while an election is held to appoint a new National Assembly, and by extension, a new Prime Minister.

At various times, Timko and his ultra-conservative, Reformed Fidesz party have threatened to pull Hungary out of the UN, the EU, NATO and the 'Treaty on the Non-Proliferation of Nuclear Weapons'. Polling of eligible voters indicates that continued participation in the European Union may be a *bona fide* point of contention in the upcoming election, as well as the potential participation in the proposed ZONT-2 space umbrella and solar power generating facility.

46

NEWS FLASH:

Budapest, Hungary, January 21, 2042, 10:51 GMT: Freeworld Press is reporting that, based on direct forensic evidence, the former Prime Minister of Hungary, Farkas Timko, and his presumed mistress, Jolan Puskas, were poisoned by a Novochok-type of nerve agent.

In sufficient dosages, these chemical agents can cause rapid respiratory and cardiac arrest and sometimes lead to a preliminary misdiagnosis of death by asphyxiation. Novochok-type nerve agents were first developed in the former Soviet Union. It is thought that both Russia and Iran have produced variants of the poison. Both Russia and Iran have denied any involvement in the murder of Timko and Puskas.

Jolan Puskas was recently hired as a server by the Buda Castle Restaurant, which is adjacent to the National Assembly Building in Budapest. Only high-ranking Hungarian government officials are allowed to make reservations in the restaurant. It is unknown what kind of relationship Jolan Puskas had with the deceased former Prime Minister. Her family, friends and colleagues refuse to talk to Freeworld Press. Budapest City Police have only revealed that she was eighteen years old and single.

The wife of Farkas Timko is also still refusing to talk to reporters.

Recently reinstated President Deco Fekete told Freeworld Press, "The nation of Hungary mourns the loss of Prime Minister Farkas Timko. When a new National Assembly has been elected, and a new Prime Minister has been appointed, a full investigation into his murder will be conducted. Make no mistake, the perpetrators will be discovered, and they will be held accountable for their actions. Every act of evil must be met with fair and just retribution.

"Although many of the Prime Minister's actions while in office were controversial, including the elimination of the position of the President of the Republic of Hungary, no one doubts that he was a patriot who thought he was doing his best for his country.

"I want to assure the other members of the EU, NATO, the UN, and the signatories to the Treaty on the Non-Proliferation of Nuclear Weapons, that Hungary will be stable and fully functional under my interim leadership. During the upcoming election, I am hopeful that voters will make the right choices and elect a National Assembly that believes it is best to fully restore our former European and global allegiances. Hungary needs to reaffirm its desire to have close alliances with our friends, while assuring our neighbouring countries, and trading partners and competitors, that we mean them no harm and are not planning any acts of aggression against them."

47

At 10:45 GMT on February 27, 2042, after surrendering his briefcase at the front desk for 'security reasons', Timofey Semenov was ushered into what a security guard referred to as a 'break-out room' in the Berlaymont office building in Brussels, Belgium. He sat there alone while waiting for the President of the European Commission, Geerten De Vries, to arrive for a scheduled meeting.

When De Vries finally arrived, about thirty minutes late, she offered no explanation or apology. She wordlessly shook Timofey's hand without much enthusiasm. Then they sat down on hard, uncomfortable chairs with a small, round, table between them.

"I hope I understand you better than your American colleague," De Vries began abruptly in Dutch-accented English. "At least you are not wearing a cowboy hat."

"No, I am not, or a Russian *ushanka* either," Timofey replied, in British-sounding English, with suppressed anger. He was not expecting to be treated with so much disrespect.

"What is this *ushanka* you are talking about?"

"It is a fur hat with ear flaps that one can tie down in the cold and the wind."

"I suppose they might be somewhat useful in Siberia, but they certainly would look silly here. Now, enough small talk, what do you want with the European Commission?"

"I was hoping we could update each other on events that might have a bearing on the ZONT-2 project."

"I see. That is the space umbrella and solar power plant gambit. Or perhaps it is simply a ruse to fleece European nations of their hard-earned cash? It still strikes me as a 'Star Wars' fantasy. And something that could be used to conduct an actual star war."

"Well, thirty-six non-Eu nations do not view it that way. And they believe, as we believe, that the rigidly-defined UN oversight role will prevent our facility from ever being used as a spaced-based weapon."

"So, you are telling me you have now signed up sufficient countries to sanction your fantastic scheme?"

"Yes, we have the Memorandums of Understanding in place. They are all based on the premise that the member nations of the European Union, as an aggregate group, or a pseudo-nation I suppose, will become a Tier One participant in the project's Stage One, together with the United States and China."

"Well, that would certainly be our rightful place."

"So, what exactly is holding back the European Commission from also executing a Memorandum of Understanding on behalf of the EU nations?"

"Well, it used to be Hungary's outrageous demands for unrelated concessions. But the new minority government there has just removed those conditions. It seems there is popular support now in Hungary for participation in your project."

"That is very good to hear. And now, what are the remaining obstacles?"

"And now, since it seems the UK will be able to appoint a representative to the ZONT-2 board of directors, France and Germany want the same power."

"France and Germany would have to become participants outside of the European Union to be able to do that. Are they proposing to leave the European Union?"

"Not in the slightest."

"So, you have lost influencing power with France and Germany?"

"Not at all. Polling indicates the voters in France and Germany are strongly in favour of participating in the space umbrella project, even if that means it must be under the EU umbrella. Please excuse the pun."

"It is a good pun. So, all you will have to do is pull some political levers, and France and Germany will come along?"

De Vries paused for a long moment. Suddenly she smiled a bit and said, "Now we are coming to the heart of it, Mister Semenov. You see, I am greatly in favour of EU participation in ZONT-2. But I think we will need two things for me to be able to successfully pull the right levers.

"First, there are no named deserts in Europe to speak off, other than some wide open, arid spaces in places like central Spain. Europe will want to have beamed power receiving stations like every other participant, if not in Stage One, then in Stage Two at the latest. European countries, including France and Germany, have many unmanned offshore wind power facilities. It would make participation much more amenable if a few of those facilities could be expanded or modified to also function as a power receiving station. The connection to an electrical power grid would also already be in place, with all the regulatory approvals and proper environmental assessments completed. The power link could be readily expanded. Would this be technically possible?"

"Yes, notionally."

"Then to give me another lever to pull, would the ZONT-2 Corporation be able to detail such a scheme?"

"Yes, without a doubt, to whatever extent required, even to naming specific facilities, and detailing what would need to be done to them exactly."

"Okay. Please make that happen, Time is of the essence. Now, the second thing I need is your help to squash a rumour that is circulating on social media. The rumour is that Europe will have to change the nature of its electrical power grids to conform to American standards. In other words, a complete change of voltages throughout our grid will be required, together with changes to the drop-down, household and industry, alternating current frequencies. Is there any truth to these rumours?"

"None at all. We will be more than willing to lay that all out for you, again to whatever extent you think is necessary."

"Then please make that happen too. And again, time is of the essence."

"Why exactly is time of the essence?"

De Vries paused for another long moment. Then she smiled again and said, "Because running the European Commission, and by extension the European Union, is like herding cats or roping goats. I see a window of opportunity right now, but our windows tend to open and shut on their own, with inexplicable, ghost like hands constantly at work. We have to deal with a moody, sometimes irrational population, with many ethnic differences."

"I understand, and I greatly sympathise with your position. We will do whatever it takes to help you get the closure of the window we both want. Oh, and please excuse my pun or metaphor this time."

"I enjoyed your pun. And thank you, Mister Semenov. This has been a most illuminating and constructive, albeit by necessity, unfortunately, a brief discussion. And I apologize for starting out so coldly. I find it a useful way to expeditiously achieve results, that is all."

"There is no need to apologize, Madame President. I thank you very much for your time today. Could you alert the senior technical members of your staff that we will soon be in touch with them? We will need some rather detailed information before we can in turn give you what you require."

"Yes, no problem, I suspected you would need to follow-up that way. I really have to run. Have a nice day."

"You, too. And goodbye."

48

It was eight o'clock in the morning on May 5, 2042. Timofey Semenov welcomed Jorge Ramirez on to his luxurious private rail car in the Kievsky Railway Station in Moscow. The two men knew their journey to the west would take a couple of days, as the car would need to be shunted between passenger trains and railway sidings. But they were both looking forward to some long overdue rest and relaxation.

Timofey was exhausted from the onerous work of helping Holt Carson and his team put in place individual ZONT-2 Stage One capital investment and revenue/power sharing contracts with thirty-seven countries, which included the EU as a pseudo-country. He had leaned heavily on his COO, Yevgeny Orlov, to complete this iterative work, but it had proven a strain for two competent executives and their large teams of equally competent professionals.

And Jorge was exhausted from just driving himself along in his regular routine as the CEO of a super-giant corporation. But he had added to his considerable workload by personally leading the effort to secure roughly seventy percent of the software, artificial intelligence, cloud, and cybersecurity ZONT-2 Stage One subcontracts.

Timofey and Jorge were now close friends, or as close as two very busy CEOs could be. They had enjoyed some whirlwind, fly-in, two-day, salmon fishing trips together, one in Labrador and one in Kamchatka. And then Timofey had invited Jorge to visit one of his sister's biodynamic farms with him. The farm was about four hundred and eighty kilometres west of Moscow. Incredibly, they determined that the five-day round trip could also fit into Jorge's tight schedule due to some last-minute overseas meeting cancellations.

And Alain Dufort and Jorge Ramirez were also developing a friendship of sorts. Alain realized that Freeworld Press was owned by Jorge, and the organization had functioned, without prompting, as both a supportive media outlet and an industrial spying organization. Timofey agreed with Alain that Jorge must have been secretly working behind the scenes to move the project along. But neither man felt the need to potentially embarrass Jorge by asking him directly to reveal the truth.

Holt Carson was still extremely busy with his large staff in the ZONT-2 Corporation's expanded headquarters in Austin, Texas. The firm had gone ahead on speculation of project approval and designed and built all the components for the ALINA-2 and ALINA-3 orbital space factories; six more uprated *Sluga*-type robotic service attendants for the L1 construction site; three geosynchronous Earth-orbiting, energy-beam, relay satellites; the modules required to build a Moon-based power relay station; and two beefed up *Lagrange* class shuttle/transport vessels to move materials from the three ALINA factories to the L1 construction site. It was now just a matter of launching everything into Earth orbit for final assembly and or commissioning. India, China, Russia and Wardenclyffe's EU-based and US-based rocket-launching companies, had all won Stage One Earth-to-orbit payload launch subcontracts.

Alain Dufort had focussed his so-called spare time on successfully obtaining an enabling UN General Assembly resolution, or the space law that would allow ZONT-2 to be built and operated at the Lagrange-1 point between the Earth and the Sun. The UN resolution would also detail how the L1 facility, relay satellites, Moon base, and Earth-based power receiving stations would be regulated. It also described the governance role that the ZONT-2 Corporation's board of directors would fulfill. And it specified which twelve countries would be empowered to appoint directors, who would in turn be accountable to the majority views of countries in defined regions of the Earth.

Alain had leaned heavily on the professional services of Emma Baumgartner for this gruelling, iterative and largely diplomatic work. She basically lived on one of Alain's hydrogen-powered, business jets with her husband as they travelled continuously around the world. Emma's husband had taken a leave of absence from his executive banking position in Switzerland to accompany his wife, and to help her out.

Alain had also stayed in close touch with Mei Wu-Toussaint. She admitted to being a spy for the Chinese government, but they remained close platonic friends. And when China, the US and the EU nations were fully onboard, in that order, Mei had worked in parallel with Alain and Emma to lobby countries, and the UN administrative organization, to structure a resolution that might enlist the required General Assembly majority support.

Timofey knew Emma was in New York for the ZONT-2 resolution vote that was scheduled for the General Assembly. The timing of the vote was uncertain, as the UN was notorious for rescheduling votes at the last minute for a myriad of sometimes dubious reasons.

Timofey had no idea what Alain was currently working on, or where he was physically located in the world. They had not talked for a few weeks. He was pleased when Alain called him on his cybersecure, combination cell and satellite phone, when he and Jorge were one day into their train journey to the west, and their vacation together.

Alain asked Timofey what he was up to. When Timofey explained the details, incredibly Alain asked if he could join them for the six-hour visit to his sister's farm. Alain said he wasn't especially interested in biodynamic farming, but he thought they should be together, if possible, should the UN vote go ahead as scheduled. Timofey wholeheartedly agreed. So, Alain said he would divert the jet he was on from its Bucharest destination to Moscow's Vnukovo Airport, where he could charter a helicopter to complete the journey. The idea was they would all meet up together at the same time at the farm.

Timofey and Alain were met at a rural Russian train station by Timofey's personal security guard and driver, Igor Garin. Igor was driving an electric UAZ-8 off-road, one-tonne, pick-up truck with an extended cab. It was basically a clone of a GM, rancher-style, pick-up truck, built under licence by the Ural Automobile Factory. It was a pleasant, although bumpy, eighteen-kilometre-long drive to the farm over gravel and sometimes dirt roads.

It was a sunny, mid-spring day, and wildflowers were starting to appear. There had been plenty of rain recently, and it was unseasonably warm. This was one of the few places on the planet where climate change may have improved things on a micro scale.

When they approached the farm, they could see that Alain was already there. A red Kazan Ansat II helicopter was parked near the unpainted, two century old, wooden farmhouse. The wood on the rambling, one-storey building was a uniform, pleasant, grey colour, and it was essentially petrified. Alain was talking to Timofey's sister, Ulyana Mikhailovna, in broken English. Alain's bodyguard, Benoit Duplantier, was standing beside the helicopter talking to the two uniformed pilots, also in broken English.

Timofey introduced Jorge to his sister. She was two years older than Timofey, but she looked to be at least five years younger. She had perfectly smooth skin, and a healthy, rosy, complexion. She was obviously fit and strong from years of physically intensive farm work. She admitted her English was not very good, so Timofey functioned as both guide and interpreter. Ulyana drove the UAZ-8 with Alain, Timofey and Jorge as passengers, and Igor followed in an UAZ-4 electric jeep with Benoit. The two pilots remained with their parked bird.

The two-hundred-hectare farm was breathtaking in its natural beauty. Ulyana said that about twenty percent of the farm's bounded area had either been left in its natural state or returned to nature. She said they grew over one hundred different types of vegetables and seventy-five varieties of stone fruit. There were contented and healthy-looking domestic animals everywhere, either in green, lush, large fields or smaller, fenced-off areas with abundant feed and water troughs. Ulyana pointed out fields of alfalfa growing next to fields of kernza, a perennial wheatgrass that was recently developed in the US state of Kansas. Kernza grain made excellent bread when mixed with conventional types of wheat and other ancient, domesticated grains.

The farm raised domestic pigs, chickens, sheep, goats, ducks, geese, horses and Scottish Highland cattle. The manure they all produced was essential for the farm's sustainability. There was also abundant wildlife that included rabbits, hares, foxes, lynx, feral domestic cats, deer, squirrels, chipmunks, birds of all kinds, and seasonally, wild ducks and geese. The large and healthy cat population kept the vermin population down. There were also English sheep dogs at work, constantly trying to maintain some sort of order, and they had been trained not to kill anything. And there were numerous ponds and a few streams with healthy native fish and amphibian populations.

The visitors talked briefly with Ulyana's middle-aged, Georgian husband, Davit. He was shoeing work horses in a well-equipped, electrified, blacksmith shed. He was a burly, friendly giant sort of guy.

Ulyana said all the animals had figured out how to coexist in a population balance with the food the farm produced. Alain jokingly suggested that the farm resembled Orwell's transitional and utopian *Animal Farm* before the Stalinist pigs took over. The others were prepared to laugh at Alain's observant analogy but held back when it seemed Ulyana did not care for the joke. Many people in Russia still considered Stalin a hero for whipping Hitler, even though his ruthless methods to consolidate power had hurt and killed many Russians.

Ulyana went on to explain that there was a lot of highly nutritious food left over for sale as well. The farm supplied markets out to a twenty-kilometre radius. There were no weeds evident anywhere, and Ulyana was adamant that no pesticides, artificial fertilizers, or herbicides had been used since the farm was first certified by Demeter as biodynamic twenty-five years before.

After the off-road tour in the two vehicles, Ulyana thought her visitors might just want to walk around a while, relax a bit, and poke their noses into the most interesting places, while she and her daughter made them a nice lunch. She said she would ring a brass cowbell when it was time to eat.

The three executives and the two bodyguards walked around the house out to a kilometre or so, and they found there were indeed lots of interesting places to explore. The compost and manure pits and bins, produce-drying and storage sheds and bins, greenhouses, and tanks of Steiner preparations, were all a bit smelly but very intriguing. Timofey explained the intricacies of how a farm like this worked, with healthy bacterial decomposition at the heart of it all, and all the men, including Alain and the two bodyguards, seemed impressed.

When the loud bell rang, the visiting men, including the bodyguards, cleaned themselves up in an entrance-way mud room and then went inside the farmhouse. They sat down in a rustic dining room right beside an ancient, large and efficient kitchen. Ulyana and her grown-up daughter Veronika heaped the table with plates of hot dishes. They also opened bottles of red and white Georgian wine for them, and filled their glasses with cold spring water.

Ulyana apologized that it was too early in the spring for fresh fruits and vegetables. Then she refused Timofey's plea for her to join the men for their meal. She insisted she and her daughter had lots of farm chores to perform, and besides, they had already eaten, and would therefore leave the men alone to discuss their many important business dealings. And she said she and Veronika just *had* to take some *proper* food out to the two obviously poorly nourished helicopter pilots.

The food was superb. Even though it had been frozen, dried, smoked, canned or otherwise preserved, the exquisite taste and high nutritional content of the many types of vegetables had not diminished. Many types of grain had been incorporated into rolls, breads, pastas and pastries. The many types of fresh and preserved meats were unlike anything one could buy from a supermarket. They were rich in good, healthy oils, low in salt and lean, and some of it was wild. And Timofey explained Ulyana was the modern Russian equivalent of a cordon bleu chef, and all her grown-up daughters were well along the same continuum.

The men were passing around the wine bottles to finish them off, when Alain's combination cell and satellite phone rang. He looked at the display, and said with a frown, "That's Emma, from New York." The two guards instantly rose to leave the dining room, but Alain politely motioned them back into their seats. So, they all were able to hear his end of the conversation:

"Hello, Emma. What's happening?"

A long three minutes elapsed while Alain just listened very carefully. They all watched his face intently. At first, he looked a bit anxious, and then he looked very tense, and then his face went completely blank. Then he said mechanically, "Thanks, Emma. And what will you and your husband be doing now?" He paused. "Oh, very good. Yes, no need to rush anywhere for a while, that's for sure. Take a bit of a break, why don't you?" His face remained neutral and unreadable while he listened to her reply. Then he said calmly, "Yes, that's a good idea too, so call me when you get there. Thanks again. And bye for now."

Alain ended the connection, and just sat there looking a bit dazed with the compact phone in his hand. Timofey gave him a few moments, and then he asked quietly, "Is anything wrong, Alain?"

Alain did not seem to hear the question. He looked at all of the other men one at a time, then he sighed, and said, "No, no. It's all good, but it was a near thing. A *very* near thing. The UN resolution passed by fifty percent plus two votes. My God, it only passed by two votes!"

Timofey stood up and yelled, "But, Alain, it *passed*, man! It is a *freaking done deal*!"

"Yes, Alain, and Timofey, it's really going to happen!" Jorge hollered as he stood up as well. "ZONT-2 is *finally* a reality! You two guys did it! Congratulations to the both of you!"

"Yes, well done, boss," Igor shyly stammered to Timofey.

Benoit simply nodded at Alain with a silly grin on his face.

Alain remained seated, sighed again, and said quietly, "Well, Timofey, it's probably time for that toast we talked about a long time ago."

Jorge and Timofey looked at Alain closely. His face looked careworn and much older suddenly. They both had known other self-driven people like Alain. They knew there was often shock and trauma when big dreams suddenly came to fruition or ended catastrophically. Obsessive executives like Alain would be lost until they could find a new megaproject to pursue. But invariably, in time, people like Alain would indeed find or create that next big challenge.

But Timofey decided he was not going to let Alain's temporary malaise spoil this magical moment. He said with a big grin, "Right you are. I'll be right back, fellows."

He came back in a few minutes from the kitchen with a frosty, unopened bottle of vodka, and five crystal tumblers, on a traditionally painted, Russian, wooden tray. He showed everyone the bottle and said in a fake deep bass voice in Russian, "*Eta Novaya Stolichnaya, Russkaya, ochen kholodnaya, vodka.*" He and Igor laughed, and then Timofey said in English, "That's the way they advertise this stuff in Moscow on the radio. It means this is new, and I'll add improved, Capital City, Russian and very cold vodka. I'll pour everyone a good shot. Remember, this stuff is meant to be sipped and savoured, not gulped."

When everyone was holding their quarter-filled tumbler of vodka in their hand, Timofey asked, "Should we all toast to ZONT-2 now?"

Jorge quickly said, "Wait." And then after a moment of thought with his eyes angled up at the ceiling, he suggested, "How about... to ZONT-2 *and beyond*? This type of farm we are visiting today is clearly in the realm of the beyond. Together with ZONT-2, they offer real hope for a better future for humanity, and the other forms of life on our planet."

For the first time, Alain smiled and said, "Yes, that's the one. Let's toast to ZONT-2 and beyond. And then to peace and friendship."

They all touched glasses, and toasted to ZONT-2 and beyond, and took a sip of vodka. Then they toasted to peace and friendship and took another sip of vodka. The solemnity of the moment was not lost on anyone. A moment of silence followed spontaneously.

Then to break the ice, Timofey laughed heartily, and said, "You know, that was an old Soviet-era toast, *Za Mir ee Droozhba*, To Peace and Friendship! But whatever. It's a good toast."

Then Timofey noticed Alain had gone quiet again, and had lapsed into some sort of sad, internal dialogue. So, he asked him quietly, "Alain, why don't you ride back on the train to Moscow with me and Jorge? It will be just the three of us on a two-day vacation away from everything. We can talk about whatever, or nothing at all. There's plenty of security. You can send Benoit back on the chopper. Or bring him along if you want."

Alain only hesitated a moment, before replying with a wavering smile, "You know, that's *exactly* what I need. Thanks, Timofey, my very close friend."